Maisey Yates is a *New York Times* bestselling author of over seventy-five romance novels. She has a coffee habit she has no interest in kicking, and a slight Pinterest addiction. She lives with her husband and children in the Pacific Northwest. When Maisey isn't writing she can be found singing in the grocery store, shopping for shoes online and probably not doing dishes. Check out her website: maiseyyates.com.

THE SPANIARD'S STOLEN BRIDE

MAISEY YATES

MILLS & BOON

First Published in Great Britain 2019
by Mills & Boon, an imprint of HarperCollins*Publishers*
1 London Bridge Street, London, SE1 9GF

© 2019 Maisey Yates

ISBN: 978-0-263-07920-3

MIX
Paper from
responsible sources
FSC˚ C007454

This book is produced from independently certified FSC™ paper
to ensure responsible forest management.
For more information visit www.harpercollins.co.uk/green.

Printed and bound in Great Britain
by CPI Group (UK) Ltd, Croydon, CR0 4YY

CHAPTER ONE

DIEGO NAVARRO HAD a bad habit of breaking his toys.

It had started with a little wooden truck when he was a boy. He hadn't intended to break it, but he'd been testing the limits, running behind it while he pushed it down on the ground.

He'd ended up falling on top of it and splitting his lip open, as well as popping the wheels off his favorite possession.

His mother had picked him up and spoken softly to him, brushing the tears from his face and taking the pieces of the truck into her hand, telling him it was okay.

His father had laughed.

He'd pushed Diego's mother aside and taken the toy from her hand.

Then he'd thrown it into the fire.

"When something is broken," he'd said darkly, "you must learn to let it go."

Those words had echoed in Diego's head later. When his mother was dead and his father stood emotionless over her body, laid out for burial before the funeral.

Diego hated his father.

He was also much closer to being his father than he would ever be to resembling his sweet, angelic mother, who had been destroyed by the hands of the man who had promised to love her.

Her hands had been gentle. Diego's were weapons of destruction.

All throughout his life he had demonstrated that to be the truth.

In a fit of frustrated rage after his mother's death, he had burned down his father's shop at the family *rancho*. His father had known he'd done it, and Diego had wondered if the old man would finally kill him too. Send him to the devil, as he had sent Diego's mother to the angels.

It had been worse. His father had simply looked at him, his dark eyes regarding him with recognition.

To be recognized by a monster as being one of his own had been a fate near death. At least then.

Diego had spent the next few years accepting it. And daring the darkness inside of him.

His father gave him a sports car for his eighteenth birthday. Diego crashed it into a rock wall on a winding road. If he had spun another direction before the accident he would have simply plummeted into the sea, and both he and the car would have sunk down to the ocean floor.

It would have been a mercy. For him to die young like that. Before he could create the kind of damage he had been seemingly destined for.

But no. He had been spared.

His mother, sweet and worthy, had not been. Reinforcing his faith in nothing other than the cruelty of life.

While he seemed to create a swath of destruction around him, Diego had thus far been indestructible himself.

It was the things he touched that burned. That broke.

Like Karina.

His one and only attempt at human connection.

His brother, Matías, was a good man. He always had been. Just as Diego had been born with a darkness in him, Matías seemed to have an innate morality that Diego could never hope to understand, much less possess.

Once he had realized that, he had isolated himself from his brother as well.

But he had met Karina. Pretty, vivacious and exciting.

She had lived life harder and faster than he had. Embracing all manner of mood-altering substances and wild sex. For a hedonist such as himself, she had been a magical, sensual embodiment of everything he hoped to lose himself in.

He had married her. Because what better way to tie his favorite new toy to him forever than through legal means?

Sadly, he had broken her too.

She had been beautiful. And he regretted it.

More than that, he regretted the life lost along with hers. The only innocent party in their entire damaged marriage.

But he was not heartbroken. He did not possess the ability to suffer such a thing.

His heart had already been broken. Shattered neatly, like his mother's bones when she had fallen off her horse after his father had shot her.

The only good thing about that was, now that it was done, it could not be done again.

Now there was only the destruction he caused the world to concern himself with.

And truly, he did not concern himself with it overmuch.

He carried those losses on his shoulders. Felt the weight of them. Like a dark and heavy cloak.

It was his nature. And he had grown to accept it.

He took a long drink of the whiskey in his hand and looked around the room. He was back at Michael Hart's impossibly stuffy New England mansion, playing the game that the older man demanded he play before they entered into any kind of business deal.

While Diego had a reputation as more of a gambler than a businessman, the truth of the matter was, he had not made his billions in Monte Carlo. He was a brilliant investor, but he made sure to keep his actions on the down low. He preferred his outrageousness in the headlines, not his achievements.

He wanted a piece of Michael Hart's company. But more than that…

He was fascinated by the man's daughter.

The beautiful heiress Liliana Hart had fascinated him from the moment he had first seen her, over two years ago. Delicate and pale, with long, white blond hair that seemed to glow around her head like a halo.

She was lovely, and nothing at all like the stereotype of an American heiress. No sky-high heels and dresses that made the wearer look most suited to dancing on poles.

She was demure. Lovely. Like a rose. He wanted to reach out and touch her, though he knew that if he did, he was just as likely to bruise her petals as anything else.

But he was not a good man. He was selfish and vain. He was also competitive. And at the moment he and his brother were being pitted against each other by their grandfather for the inheritance of the family *rancho*.

They had to marry to get their share or forfeit entirely.

Matías was too good to rush out and pluck a wife out of thin air simply for financial gain.

Diego wasn't too good for anything. He would happily marry a woman for financial gain. And if on top of it, Liliana made his blood pound in a way no other woman ever had.

The money was an aside. The real attraction was besting his brother, and debauching Liliana.

And if Michael Hart was willing to give her up in trade for his investment in the company and solve the issue of his inheritance along with it?

Diego would chance bruising her.

He would be more annoyed with his *abuelo* if the old man's edict hadn't given him the excuse he'd needed to pursue the beautiful jewel of a woman who had captured his eye from the first.

He saw a flash of pink by the library door, and he realized it was Liliana, peeking inside, and then running away.

A smile curved his lips. He knocked the rest of the whiskey back, and then excused himself from the gathering, striding out with confidence, enough that no one asked where he was going.

No one dared question him.

He saw her disappear around the corner, and he followed, his footfall soft on the Oriental rug that ran the length of the hall.

There was a door slightly ajar, and he pushed it open, finding that it was another library. And inside, standing behind one of the wingback chairs, her delicate hands resting on the back, was Liliana.

"Ms. Hart," he said. "We have not had a chance to say hello to each other tonight."

Her face went scarlet. He found it so incredibly appealing. She always blushed when they talked. Because she found him beautiful. He was not a man given to false humility. Or indeed, humility of any kind.

God had made him beautiful, and he well knew it. But God had also made vipers beautiful. The better to attract their prey.

The fact he knew the weapons at his disposal was more necessity than vanity.

That Liliana found herself under his spell would make this so much easier.

"Mr. Navarro. I didn't realize... That is... I don't make a habit of attending my father's business parties."

"You attended our business dinner only a few weeks ago."

She looked down. "Yes. That's different."

"Is it? I'm tempted to believe that you're avoiding me, *tesoro*."

"What does that mean?" she asked.

"Treasure," he said, taking a step toward her.

"And why would you call me that?"

He paused, midstride. She was not exactly what she appeared. Or perhaps she was. There was an openness to her. A lack of fear that spoke most certainly of inexperience. At least, inexperience with men like him.

Are there men like you? Or just monsters?

"It is what you are, is it not? Certainly, you are a treasure to your father."

"If by that you mean a commodity."

A smile curved his lips. "Well, money is the way of the world."

"It would be nice if it weren't."

"Spoken like a woman who has always had it." It wasn't the first time he'd stolen time away to speak with Liliana. He found himself drawn to her like a magnet. And no amount of pursuing other women had dampened his interest in her.

"I prefer books," she said, those delicate fingers curling around the chair, as if she were using it to brace herself.

"I prefer to experience life, rather than hiding away in a dusty library with only fantasy to entertain me."

She surprised him by rolling her eyes. "Yes. A man of action. I prefer to pause and learn about the world, rather than simply wrapping myself up in my own experiences."

"I didn't realize you were socially conscious," he said.

"A terrible detraction from my charms. Or so I'm told."

He took another step toward her. "Who has told you this?"

"My father."

"He is incorrect," Diego said. "I find it fascinating."

"Well. In that case. All of my personal issues of self-worth are solved."

"I'm glad I could help."

They stared at each other and he felt something. Heat. But something deeper. He was well acquainted with sexual attraction, and much in defiance of his typical fare, Liliana had an innocence about her that should not appeal to him. But did.

Still, he could appreciate the fact that his appetite—jaded from years of gluttony—was interested in something a bit different.

Something softer, sweeter.

She was like a ripe strawberry. And he wanted badly to have a bite.

But that thing beneath it... That current that made him feel as though he was being drawn to her against his will; that he could not quite understand.

She looked away, and her glossy hair caught the firelight, shimmering orange, as though the flames had wrapped themselves around the silken strands.

He closed the distance between them, and she did not turn to look his way. He reached out, brushing her curls to one side, his fingertips brushing the delicate skin of her neck.

"You are truly beautiful, Liliana. Do you know that?"

She looked at him, those blue eyes guarded. "Men have told me that before. Usually when they want something from my father."

"Is that so?" It was on the tip of his tongue to tell her that he wanted something from her father too. That he wanted her. But he held it back.

"My father is a powerful man."

"So am I, *tesoro*." He placed his hand on her hip and felt a jolt beneath his touch. "Believe me when I tell you that I do not require anything to help bolster that. I need a hand up from no one. My money is my own, and my power is my own."

"Is it?" she whispered.

"What do you think of that?"

She reached up, as though she were going to touch his face, and then she jerked her hand away. "Your power's all your own?"

"Perhaps at the moment some of it is with you."

She jerked away from him suddenly, almost tipping toward the fireplace before he caught her around the waist and sent them both stumbling back against the rock fireplace. His chest was pressed against her breasts, and she was breathing hard, those blue eyes locked with his.

"Sorry," she said, breathless.

She began to wiggle, trying to get out of his hold.

"You don't really want to escape me," he whispered.

"I have to. I was avoiding you."

"And I found you."

"Don't you want to know why?"

There was something in her voice, a catch in her tone that made him find he did want to know. He released his hold and took a step back. And that was when he noticed the sparkling diamond on her left hand.

"Why, Liliana?" he asked.

"I told you, a great many men have seen me as a way to get to my father."

"So you did."

"And, well… One of them presented him with an offer that neither of us could refuse."

"Is that so?" he asked, his voice rough, raging heat and fire and fury burning inside of him. "That is so interesting, as your father did not indicate as much to me."

"Were you bartering with my father for my body as well?"

"Yes," he responded.

He did not tell her that he had been offering her father money, and not the other way around. That he wanted her most of all.

"You're not different," she said, turning away from him. "Which is good to know."

"It doesn't matter. I doubt we'll ever see each other again."

She laughed softly. "We probably will. Christmases. Birthdays. That sort of thing."

"Why would we see each other then?"

"Because, Diego. I'm about to become your sister-in-law. I'm marrying your brother."

CHAPTER TWO

SHE WAS GETTING MARRIED. She could hardly believe it.

Liliana had spent her life being cosseted and protected in her family's sprawling estate in the US. While she had done a bit of traveling, it had always been under the watchful eye of her father and the au pair he had chosen to keep her company.

This was the first time in her life she'd felt like she wasn't being hovered over.

She had been in Spain now for two weeks with her fiancé, Matías.

Fiancé.

It was so very strange.

She had spent more time talking to…

She swallowed hard, curling her hands into fists as she sat down on the edge of the bed in her room.

She tried not to think of those piercing, dark eyes. That rakish grin that looked like dangerous enticement.

Truly, Matías and Diego Navarro looked so much alike it shouldn't make one bit of difference to her which one she married. They were both devastatingly handsome. And by all accounts, Matías was a much better man than his brother. Not that she knew much about them. She refused to allow herself to search the internet for information about Diego, as much as she had wanted to. But he radiated an air of danger that Matías simply did not.

That was the problem. There was something more than looks driving that strange connection she had felt to Diego from the moment she had first set eyes on him two years earlier. She'd heard people describe attraction in terms of being struck by lightning.

She'd met Diego Navarro and it had been as if a black fire had been lit inside her. Burning slowly, growing, over the course of all that time.

Matías was a good man. A man that her father wanted to do business with. And why shouldn't she…

Why shouldn't she do exactly as he asked?

After all, she was the reason he had lost the love of his life. The reason her fragile, beautiful mother had died in childbirth.

She had to be the daughter her mother would have wanted. A daughter who was worth the loss her father had sustained. A daughter who made him happy. A daughter who was enough.

And so she did her best.

She had always known that her father would have a hand in choosing her husband.

She had accepted it with grace and dignity. The only time she had ever mouthed off, the only time she had ever allowed the witch rolling around in her mind to escape, was in conversation with Diego.

There was no point thinking about him now.

He had not offered for her.

But he might have.

She closed her eyes and sighed.

She heard footsteps in the hall and her heart rate quickened. She sat there on the edge of the bed, praying that it wasn't Matías.

There was no reason to believe that it should be.

Two weeks she had been here, and he hadn't so much as kissed her.

He had been solicitous beyond the point of reason. Constantly putting parasols over her head in the sun and worrying over her pale skin in the heat. Like she was a scoop of ice cream that might melt into a puddle.

She might be free of her father, but her fiancé had taken up the charge of overprotective presence easily enough.

Today had been the first time he had given her a bit of breathing room. There had been an accident with one of the horses on the *rancho* and a stable boy, and Matías had been consumed with the care of the boy since it had happened. As a result, Liliana had finally been given a few hours free to wander the *rancho* without someone clucking after her like a hen.

That was what was so funny. He was more like a protective older brother than he was a fiancé. At least, how she would imagine a fiancé would be.

And she was grateful for it. Which was another bad sign, she imagined.

She had never seen a married couple together. She didn't know how her parents had been, but the way that her father talked about her mother made her believe that theirs had been a passionate love. That when she had died his heart had been ripped from his body and sent to the grave right along with her.

She couldn't imagine having a connection like that with another person.

Much less Matías.

She didn't think she wanted one like that, really.

The footsteps passed by and she let out a sigh of relief. She wasn't ready to be physical with him. Which was foolish, as they were going to be married very soon. They would have to be physical then. They should kiss. *Something.* They should do something.

The idea didn't disgust her—it was just that she found...

When she closed her eyes and thought of kissing Matías, inevitably, his sculpted, dark features transformed. Into more dangerous ones.

Diego.

She had never—not in all her life before setting eyes on that man—indulged in childish infatuations. Having always had a sense that her father was going to arrange her marriage, she had known there was no point.

She wasn't a fairy-tale princess. Prince Charming wasn't going to come for her.

Prince Acceptable was going to be selected for her.

And so there had never been a crush. Never been a fantasy.

Until *him*.

She wondered if it could be called a crush or a fantasy. This dark, terrible feeling that made her want to do something reckless and awful. Something the Liliana she'd been raised to be would never consider.

Diego was the worst possible man for her to have developed a connection to. The worst possible man to be fixated on now.

Her father wanted her to do this and she'd poured all of her energy, all of her life, all of herself, into doing what he asked.

Liliana felt compelled to be a counterpoint to death. And that was a very heavy weight to carry. But she was alive. Her mother was dead.

Could she complain about anything being too heavy when she *lived*?

But you'll live your whole life without ever touching him...

"It doesn't matter!"

She hadn't meant to say that out loud, but it burst from her mouth and she looked around, hoping her voice didn't draw attention to her.

It didn't matter. *He* didn't matter.

She'd made her choices. She could have been a rebellious daughter. She could have pushed back against her father's edicts. His demands she learn etiquette and deportment instead of going on to university. His pronouncement that she'd play hostess when he had businessmen over.

His long-standing proclamation he would choose her husband.

But when she thought of rebelling against him...

It made her cold all over.

Her father was her only family. The only person in the world who loved her.

How could she push back against that? How could she test that?

Maybe someday Matías would love her.

The idea didn't fill her with any sense of joy.

She stood from the bed and paced across the large bedroom. The *rancho* was opulent, but she had spent her life surrounded by opulence. It was nothing new, and suddenly, she despised her own jadedness on that score.

So many people would be grateful to marry Matías. To be made his princess, for all intents and purposes. To be the lady of the *rancho*, and have all these beautiful lands, this incredible hacienda and the horses that came with it.

And she could find nothing, no sense of excitement, no sense of triumph inside of her.

Nothing at all.

She stood at the window, brushing the curtains to the side and looking out at the well-manicured lawn. The pale moonlight spilled over the rippling grass, the slight breeze making it look like water rather than earth. Making her feel as though she could open the window and dive straight down into the depths and swim far, far away from all of this.

Suddenly, she saw movement. Not the shift of a blade of grass, but a shadow, moving across the grounds. She didn't know what possessed her, only that she unlatched the window, opening it and the screen along with it, leaning out slightly so that she might get a better look at whatever was below.

And then, the dark shadow was closer to the house, and she could see for sure what it was.

A man.

There was a man out on the grass, moving around. She should call someone. For in all likelihood someone clearly sneaking through the property was not staff, and was not supposed to be here at all.

Perhaps he was one-half of a pair of ill-fated lovers. In which case, she didn't want to call anyone.

Her own love life was, if not ill-fated, then severely stunted, and she was hardly going to damage anyone else's.

But the figure kept coming closer to the house, and when he began to scale the side of the building, using the ornate molding and the window ledges as footholds, she stood frozen, watching him.

She should scream. She should call out for help. But she didn't. She simply stood. With the window open, as if she were inviting him in. He kept moving closer, and closer. And then he looked up, and she saw dark, glittering eyes just barely visible in the moonlight.

Still. She didn't move. Still, she stood without making a sound.

It wasn't until he climbed to her window, and wrapped his arm around her waist, one hand holding tightly to the molding up above, his eyes clashing with hers, that she screamed.

"Now we must hurry," he said, that voice low and far too familiar. "Because you have caused a scene."

She found herself being jerked from the window, suspended above the ground, terror roaring through her veins.

She clung to the man, because she had no choice. She would fall to her... Well, perhaps not her death, but her certain maiming if she did not cling to those strong, broad shoulders, her breasts pressed against the chest so solid it seemed to be made of stone rather than flesh.

But he was hot. Hot in a way that only flesh and blood could be.

He had spoken.

And she *knew*.

Knew exactly who held her in his arms.

"I have a helicopter waiting," he whispered. "Are you holding on to me?"

"Y-yes."

"Good," he responded.

He let go of her and she wrapped her arms more tightly around his neck, as he made startling time scaling down the side of the house. She gave a short prayer of thanks when her feet connected with the grass, but it was short-lived as she found herself being picked up and hauled away quickly.

She heard voices, shouting, and she looked over his

shoulder to see dark figures standing in her bedroom window. Clearly responding to the scream.

"We will escape before he manages to mobilize. Believe me. I was hardly going to plan a kidnapping that I could not execute. I'm far too vain for such a thing."

"For kidnapping?"

"For *failed* kidnappings. I would only ever engage in a successful one." He bustled her into a car waiting at the edge of the lawn and drove them to the edge of the woods, taking her out of the car again, hauling her around like she was a sack of nightgown-wearing potatoes.

"Why exactly are you kidnapping me?" she asked, as she hung limp over his shoulder.

It was strange, she imagined, that she wasn't fighting him. That she wasn't screaming or pitching a massive fit, trying to escape his hold.

But she didn't want to. Not even a little bit. Not in the slightest. She found that she wanted to…see where he was going. Because hadn't it been Diego she had just been thinking of?

And she had to ask herself why she had stood there with the window open if she truly didn't want to be taken.

And so she let him carry her into the woods, across to a clearing, where there was indeed a helicopter awaiting them. He hauled her up inside easily, depositing her in the seat and buckling her before taking his position at the controls.

"You pilot…helicopters?"

"We don't have time to talk."

He fired up the rotors, and they began to gain speed. Just as she saw lights in the distance, they lifted off from the ground, above the trees, and away.

She couldn't hear, not over the sound of the engine and the propellers, but then he put a headset on, and placed one on her head as well. She adjusted it.

"Can you hear me?"

His voice came over the speakers and into her ears. "Yes," she responded.

"Excellent."

"Did you want to make conversation now?" It seemed strange, all things considered.

"I thought we might pick up where we left off when last we spoke," he said.

"Did you? Well, it might be a slightly different conversation, Diego, as when last we spoke we were in my father's library. And today we are in a helicopter, with you having kidnapped me from my fiancé's home."

"You will not marry him."

Her heart kicked into gear, slamming into her breastbone. "I won't?"

"No," he said, his voice dark and decisive.

"He's going to come for me."

"I'm not going anywhere that he will be able to trace us. My brother and I are not close. Believe me when I tell you he has no idea of all the residences I own. Nor the aliases they are listed under."

"Aliases…"

"What did you think of me, *tesoro*? That I was simply misunderstood? And that was why I was the black sheep of the Navarro family? No. I am not misunderstood. Not in the least. In point of fact, I am rather well understood. I'm not a good man."

"That is not…overly comforting, considering I'm now hurtling through the air with you."

"It was not intended to be a comfort. I'm simply

making sure that you are aware of the position you find yourself in."

"What position is that?"

"You're going to marry *me* now, Liliana."

Something hot and reckless jolted through her, a lot like fear, but with a hard edge to it that thrilled her as much as it repelled her.

"You can't just… How can you possibly think that I would agree to that?"

"Don't be silly, *tesoro*. I have all the ammunition I could possibly want. Did you honestly think I would go to all this trouble without hedging my bets? I was not counting on my charm to sway you."

If only he knew. Before this moment, he could have climbed through the window and seduced her, likely so easily it would be humiliating.

She had never kissed a man. Not truly. The chaste exchanges she'd had with Matías were nothing like a real kiss, and the idea of Diego's lips kept her awake at night.

Indeed, they had been keeping her awake this very night. And he had no idea. Of course not.

But now… Now she was seeing him in a slightly different light.

She looked at him, his face cast in sharp relief by the glow of the control panel in front of him. High, hard-cut cheekbones, a cruel, sculpted mouth, nose straight like a blade.

Oh, dear heaven, she was no less attracted to him now than she had been before. There was perhaps something wrong with her. And she wasn't entirely certain there was anything that could be done about it. She wasn't entirely certain there was anything she would want to do about it. Because she had never felt anything like this. Nothing quite so dangerous, nothing quite so exhilarating. Her life had been lived entirely to please her father. Entirely to live up to the memory of her mother.

Lusting for dark and dangerous men fit nowhere in that. But Diego had swept into her father's house like an undeniable force. Indeed, he had swept into her bedroom tonight like one as well. And at the moment there was nothing she could do.

She was being whisked away, after all. She could hardly leap from the helicopter.

And the fact that he made her stomach sink, made it swoop like a butterfly whose wings had been torn, one that was falling out of the sky, toward its inevitable demise… Well, right now there was nothing she could do about that.

"If you truly wanted to marry me, you could have spoken to my father," she said, her voice small.

"You don't understand," Diego said. "I must prevent my brother from marrying you." He turned to face her for a moment, his lip curled into a sneer. "If he marries you, then he gains the inheritance of the ranch. I want you, and I want the *rancho*. My marriage ensures that I get it. And that is why you must marry me. The fact that I have fantasies of tearing that virginal nightgown from your body is only a bonus."

His words rolled over her like a poison. He didn't want her, not really. He didn't want to marry her because he had any finer feelings for her. He wanted to marry her because of an inheritance.

Matías wanted to use her as well, wanted to use her to forge an alliance with her father, and apparently, to get an inheritance. But that didn't bother her. Because when it came to Matías, she had only been following her father's orders.

Her feelings for Diego had nothing to do with orders.

"If my brother has had you, that makes no difference to me. In fact, I shall take a great joy in wiping your memory of him from your mind."

She realized what he meant, though it took a moment, and shock rolled over her.

She had not been with Matías. But she wasn't going to tell him that. She didn't know why, but for the moment it felt like a small bit of power.

He said that he didn't care, but the fact he had mentioned it made her think that perhaps he did.

And so she said nothing. She simply sat with her hands folded, staring straight ahead into the darkness as she was taken further and further away from any kind of certainty and deeper into this madness of Diego's making.

CHAPTER THREE

DIEGO WATCHED HIS captive closely as they walked from the helicopter toward his home. If she was expecting that there would be anyone here who might become sympathetic to her plight and offer her assistance, she would be sadly mistaken. He had taken pains to clear his house of all the usual staff, leaving it stocked with everything they would need to get through the next period of time without drawing attention to them.

He paused at the beginning of the walkway that led up to the old manor that looked near consumed by ivy where it was pressed deep into a rocky hillside.

He extended his gloved hand, and she took it, and he could feel her delicate fingers, could feel the heat of her body through the black leather.

He felt a bit like Hades, leading Persephone down into the underworld.

Some men might be consumed with guilt at that easy comparison. The idea that they might be the devil himself.

Diego suffered from no such guilt.

Diego did not suffer from a conscience at all.

Liliana was silent, and she looked like a very small ghost shrouded in her white nightgown, her pale hair blowing in the breeze.

"Where are we?"

"On a private island," he said. "Near enough to Spain, but far enough as well. This is mine. And no, my brother does not know."

"It's… It looks rather English."

"The English like Spain," he said. "At least, they like to get drunk in Spain."

"Is that what *you* like about Spain?"

"I *am* Spanish, *querida*."

"Of course," she said, her cheeks coloring slightly.

How funny that she could be embarrassed over making a faux pas with him. Her kidnapper. How charming that she would care at all.

"I take that as a compliment on the proficiency of my English," he said. His lips curved into a smile. "But not as much of a compliment on my character."

"Were you looking for compliments on your character, Diego? Because if so, you might have stopped short of the kidnapping."

He chuckled. "I was not. It is delightfully freeing when you don't care about your own morality. If you just sink into turpitude, I find that it has a very warm embrace. And there are a host of fabulous side effects. A lack of caring what anyone thinks. Least of all your own conscience."

"Some of us don't live exclusively for ourselves," she said softly.

"Your father?" He wondered if the poor creature imagined her father to be a good man. Why wouldn't she? She was… She was sweet. And in this world that was a rare and precious thing. A thing he was going to destroy. He should care about that. He found he didn't. "What a fantastic paragon for you to live for."

He began to walk more quickly, drawing her into the

entryway of the house, and pressing his thumb against the door to unlock it. "My thumbprint only, *tesoro*," he said.

"Does that include getting out as well?"

He laughed. "You know it does. Again, I would not conduct a kidnapping without being thorough."

"I suppose I should appreciate that as a commentary on my fortitude and ingenuity."

"I feel that you should be flattered by this entire caper."

"Should I?"

"Indeed. I've gone to quite a lot of trouble to procure you."

"More due to the relationship with your brother than anything to do with you."

"Yes. But if I did not find you enticing in your own right then I would simply have held on to you until the date on my grandfather's great edict expired."

"Lucky me."

"Many women would say that you were lucky. Being fought over by the Navarro brothers as you are."

"And yet, I feel more like a wretched hen between the jaws of two posturing dogs."

"Or, a precious gem being traded amongst thieves. Pick your metaphor, *tesoro*. I would pick the more flattering of the two."

"I don't have the motivation. Flattered or not, I remain kidnapped."

"Perhaps you will in time." He brought her inside, closing the door behind them. The lock clicked with a delicious, satisfying finality.

"What are you going to do with me?" For the first time, she looked afraid. No, more than afraid—terrified. And two things dawned on him in that moment.

That she had not looked truly frightened this entire time, which was an oddity. She seemed to have accepted her kidnapping with a remarkable aplomb. She had not fought him. In fact, she had clung to him, long after her safety had depended on it.

She had opened the window for him.

Something about that kicked masculine triumph through his veins. She did not hate him. That much was clear.

Or perhaps, she did not care for his brother. It didn't matter to him which it was. Not in the least. The fact that it was either was good enough.

The second was that she looked out of her mind with fear at the moment, and he did not care for that. Another revelation. He could not recall much caring about the feelings of another. Not ever.

Or at least, not in quite some time.

"I already told you," he said. "I intend to marry you."

"Are we alone here?" She backed up against the wall, her pulse thundering at the base of her throat.

Diego frowned and walked toward her, marveling as she shrank away from him, turning herself near inside out to avoid him. He reached out, pressed his thumb against that delicate hollow there. It felt like a frightened bird against his touch, fluttering, trying to escape.

"What do you think I will do to you?"

"You have already kidnapped me. I fear that any number of indignities can't be too far away."

He dropped his hand quickly. "I have never once forced myself on a woman. I would hardly start with you."

"Why do you say it like *that*?"

"Because you want me."

"I want you? You kidnapped me. Do you honestly

think that I'm panting after you now that you've stolen me out of my bedroom window?"

He lifted a brow and shrugged one shoulder. "A bedroom window you opened for me. That makes your protests slightly weak."

"I didn't know it was you."

"Did you not?"

Her shoulders went rigid. "I did not."

"It is moot. I saw the way you looked at me at your father's house. You wanted me then. You want me now. I would take absolutely no pleasure in forcing you. I would much rather you had to lower yourself to beg for what you want. Taking it from you would make it far too easy on you."

Her lip curled and she raised her hand, pulling it back as if she meant to strike him. He didn't stop her. He merely stood, ready for her strike. And she of course didn't land the blow.

It did not surprise him. Not in the least.

"A word of advice, *tesoro*," he said. "If you're going to make threats you had best be prepared to follow through. I am not a man who makes idle threats, and therefore, you do not want to be the kind of woman who makes them. Not in my presence. If you're going to hit me, you best do it hard. If you're going to tempt my retribution, then it had better be worth it."

She said nothing. She simply stood there, shaking like an indignant leaf, her rage and fear barely suppressed. "Would you like to go to your room?"

"I'll have my own room?"

He sighed heavily, feigning exasperation. "Of course you will have your own room. I already made it clear that I do not intend to force myself on you."

"You just intend to force marriage on me."

"Naturally." He said it as if it were the most obvious thing in the entire world.

"You make no sense."

"I'm a villain. I don't have to make sense."

He turned away from her and they began to walk up the long staircase and down a winding corridor, leading her to the chamber he had selected expressly for her.

Truly, the entire house had been chosen for her. The entire island.

There was something classic about it. Classic, and yet wild. He had appreciated it from the moment he'd set eyes on it last week. From the moment he had decided on his course of action.

The chamber that he had selected for her, had had furnished and decorated and filled with beautiful clothes, had been chosen specifically with her in mind. He had imagined how she might react to it. Had imagined the delight she might take in the way the soft mattress molded itself around her body, in the way the soft fabrics felt against her skin.

Instead, when she saw the room, her expression was blank.

"Is it not to your liking?"

"As jail cells go, I imagine it's quite a beautiful one."

"There is a library," he bit out. "Just through that door."

"Do you think this is a movie? And that you can buy away my ire with books?"

"You told me you liked books," he said.

"Books *and* freedom. Perhaps I should have added that last part."

"Sadly, in this instance, you may have one, but not the other."

He began to walk away, his heart thundering hard,

rage he did not quite understand beginning to spike in his system.

"How do you expect that you'll force me to marry you?" she asked. "I can't do anything about the fact that you have me in this house, but you cannot make me say vows."

He paused, bone-deep satisfaction rolling through him. "I already told you, *tesoro*. I have thought of absolutely everything."

"What have you thought of?"

"You told me that you live for other people. For your father. Well, I know things about Michael Hart that would destroy your girlish fantasies of the man you call father. I can ruin him, Liliana. His reputation, his fortune. I can reduce it all to dust."

"How? My father is a good man."

"Your father is a criminal, who has made the same mistake a great many idiotic criminals make. He has built his power upon legitimacy. For my part? I am a criminal who would lose nothing if the world were to find out."

"You could be arrested for kidnapping me."

"Could I? Do you suppose I am not prepared to bribe officials in Spain and in the United States to make sure that is not so? You mistake me for a man with limits."

"The man that I knew back at my father's home... He was not a monster."

"Yes," Diego said, advancing toward her. "He was. The monster is always there, Liliana, and make no mistake." He reached out, grabbing hold of her hand and forcing it down onto his chest, over his heart. "Understand this. No matter how civil I may seem, the monster is always there. When I'm smiling at you, the monster is there. Right there," he said, pounding her hand against him now. "Do not ever forget it."

Her eyes went wide, and for a moment he thought he might have succeeded in terrifying her. Then her face relaxed, a clear decision having taken place inside her.

"As seduction bids go," she said, her voice wobbly, "this is not a good one."

She was tough, was Liliana. Never as fragile as she appeared.

"At what point did you begin to believe this was a seduction? If I had wanted to seduce you, I would have done so back at your father's home. I could have. We both know. The moment you told me you were to marry my brother I could have had you on the floor. I can sense how badly you want me. But it's not enough. It's not permanent enough for my purposes. And that's why I didn't. I wanted insurance. And I found it. Your father has been scamming those who invest in his company. And I have the proof. Not only that, there are rafts of harassment allegations from a great many female employees. All buried. Covered up by his money. But the only person who possesses the power to pay more than he does is me. I have my finger poised on the kill button, Liliana, and he would be a fool to think I won't press it."

"He… He couldn't have."

"Oh, but he could have. And did."

"If you draw attention to yourself…"

"My reputation as a gambler, womanizer and reprobate will be compromised?"

She shrank in on herself, clearly realizing that she was defeated.

"I recommend that you get a good night's sleep. For we are to be married as quickly as possible."

"How?"

"I have already begun the paperwork for a license. It requires only your signature and then it is poised to be processed. After which I have arranged for an officiant to come and speak our vows to us. I am a traditionalist at heart. I could have simply had us married over the computer, but I find technology so cold."

"I don't think it's technology. I rather think it's your heart."

He laughed. "No, darling. I don't have a heart."

"I just felt it beating."

"You just felt the monster. Trying to escape."

CHAPTER FOUR

LILIANA WAITED UNTIL she was certain that Diego was asleep. Or, if not asleep, then not roaming the house. She needed to figure out if there was some method that she could use to contact the outside world.

In all likelihood, there wasn't.

And in fact, Diego would probably be insulted if she voiced that to him. "No, *tesoro*," she intoned in a deep voice, "I would not be so sloppy as to leave an accessible landline."

She blew out a breath and sneaked out of the bedroom, padding down the hall and then down the stairs. She knew there had to be an office down there. And perhaps, if she could find that, there would be a phone. A fax machine. Something.

She could hardly believe she had been kidnapped only a few hours ago. She felt as if it had been days. She felt as if she had been wearing this nightgown for her entire life.

She had looked in the closets and seen there were other clothes, but she hadn't been able to bring herself to put any of them on. Not even an alternate nightgown. It was too strange. She was not going to take something offered to her by a kidnapper and a blackmailer.

Her heart twisted.

That was the most difficult thing. That part of her had felt something for Diego. That she had thought there had been some mystical connection between them from the moment they'd met two years ago. And it had been a lie.

It's just the monster trying to get out.

If this was him with his monster buried, then she really wouldn't like to see him with the monster out.

She picked around the furniture downstairs, tip-toeing to one closed door after the other. Some rooms were empty, others holding dusty furniture that gave her some measure of hope. It was entirely possible he hadn't scoured the place for methods of communication.

The man who put the thumbprint reader on the door didn't look for a phone?

She ignored her mouthy inner bitch and pressed on.

She was crouched down below the desk when the door to the study opened.

"What exactly are you doing?"

She popped up, banging her head on the furniture, so hard that a white light burst behind her eyes. She rubbed at it furiously, whimpering as she tried to stand.

Suddenly, strong arms had come around her, were holding her close, pulling her against his body. "Do not hurt yourself," he growled.

Heat spread through her like a fire, the strength in his hold shocking. She forgot to breathe, her head swimming, her body going weightless and floaty. From not breathing. Not from the look in those dark, stormy eyes. Not from staring down at those sculpted lips and wondering how it would feel if they...

She took a step back, stumbling slightly, but finding balance when she was some distance from him.

"Do not startle me," she bit out.

"It was not my intention to startle you. Why are you snooping around?"

"I need to talk to my father."

He laughed. "All you had to do was say so."

"You're going to let me talk to my father?"

"I imagine you have questions for him. It behooves me that he answer them. Because I am not lying to you. I know that you wish I were. But if you need to hear it from your father himself, then by all means."

He held his cell phone out to her, and she took it, feeling suspicious. "I'm not even sure what time it is there."

"Does it matter? You have been kidnapped, after all."

"You're not worried that my father is going to call the police?"

"My brother already has."

"And you're not worried..."

"So concerned for my feelings, *tesoro*. It is admirable, and a bit touching, but there really is no need. I am more rock than man."

"Unsurprising."

She dialed her father's number, feeling self-conscious with Diego standing there staring at her. Her head still throbbed.

"Hello?"

"Father," Liliana said. "I've been kidnapped."

"How much money does he want?" her father asked, his voice clipped and tight, but not as surprised as she would've thought.

"I... He wants to marry me."

"Are you having a last-minute fit about marrying Matías?"

"No," she protested. "I'm not having a fit. I'm currently a victim of a crime."

"What?"

"I was kidnapped. I told you. From Matías's house."

"*Who* has taken you?"

"Diego. Diego Navarro."

The silence on the end of the phone suddenly became weighted. Tense. "What does he want?"

"To marry me," she reiterated. "It's complicated. But he said… He said I had to."

"Why did he say that?" The fact that her father didn't sound shocked concerned her more than just about anything else.

"He said he knows things about you. Things that could ruin you. He said… He said that he can destroy you. Your reputation. Your fortune. Everything. If it's not true…"

"You must stay with him," her father said. "You must give him what he asks for."

Liliana felt like the world had dropped out from beneath her feet. "I… You can't truly expect for me to marry my kidnapper?"

"One Navarro should be the same as the other. In any case, this one is much more dangerous."

"He *kidnapped* me."

"Has he harmed you?"

"I have been terrorized," she said, ignoring the flare of amusement in Diego's eyes when she said the word.

Honestly, she wanted to hit him.

"Has he put his hands on you in any way?" her father pressed.

"Other than when he carried me out of my bedroom window, no," she admitted, reluctant to do so, because it was clear that somehow that seemed to absolve Diego from taking her against her will.

"I cannot tell you I have no reason for concern," her father said. "I can only tell you that if you don't wish to lose absolutely everything we have… You must marry him."

"But I…"

"Your mother dearly loved our life together. She loved the company that she and I built together. To lose it would destroy her."

But she's dead. Liliana wanted to scream. She couldn't. So she didn't. Instead, she simply hung up the phone. With numb fingers, she handed it back to Diego.

"I assume he did not give you the answer that you required."

"No."

"I told you that you would not care for the answer."

Her mind was spinning. "I don't believe that you want a wife," she said finally.

"Why exactly?"

"I don't believe you want fidelity."

"Well. I've never tried it for too terribly long. But I have managed it for a couple of years, at least."

That admission surprised her. "Really?"

"It is not my past that is open for discussion. However, continue."

"I'll marry you," she said. "I will marry you for exactly as long as we have to stay married. But then, I want money. To go and live my own life. I want to be free. Of you and of my father. Let his empire stand but help me be free of it. And once you don't need me anymore…you can be free of me."

She felt exhilarated. She had never conceived of doing anything quite so reckless. Of figuring out a way to tilt the scale so that she might benefit. Freedom. Not just from her father, but from a husband.

Finding out that her father could do such a thing to her. That he could manipulate her as he was doing now, so easily. Even as he was revealing himself to be a villain, bringing up her mother's death. A death she had no control over. But one that she felt an immense amount of guilt over all the same. It was sobering. And immensely painful.

It made her reckless. It made her want something different. Made her want something more.

"I will not be satisfied with the marriage in name only," he said, his obsidian eyes dark on hers.

She was afraid his gaze would burn right through her, and that his touch would reduce her to ash. What would it be like to be naked with someone? Naked with him.

It would be so overwhelming. So intimate. So impossibly close.

She'd spent her whole life feeling close to no one. The very idea made her tremble.

She shrank back. "You said you wouldn't force yourself on me."

"And I won't. But I'm making it very clear, that while I may agree to a marriage with an end date, and while I have absolutely no issue providing you with a settlement, I do expect what I want. As I said, if I did not wish to marry you I would have simply kept you away from Matías. But I want you." He moved closer to her, reminding her of a large, dangerous cat. "I have wanted you from the moment I first laid eyes on you. Wanted to spoil all that innocent beauty that you carry around with you so effortlessly." He didn't move nearer to her. Didn't touch her. And yet she felt him. As if his words had reached inside of her. "Do you know what I mean by that?" he asked.

She was trembling. From the inside out. And frankly,

she didn't quite know what he meant by that. But she refused to look so foolish.

"I suppose you're a man. And you can't help your-self."

"Oh, it goes so far beyond me being a man and you being a woman. If it was only that, I could satisfy it with anyone. But you... You, Liliana, have bewitched me from the moment I first laid eyes on you and I find that unacceptable. I do not want without having. It is not in my nature."

What difference would it make? Really. She had been willing to sleep with Matías. But then, she had been planning on staying married to him, but truly, she had already been planning on being with a man she didn't love. Why not this one?

And you want him.

She ignored that voice.

The fact of the matter was the idea of being with him didn't... It didn't disgust her. And she was...curious. It was funny how she felt profoundly uncurious when it came to Matías. But there was something about Diego. A spark that was between them... Or at least, it lived inside of her. And it fascinated her. It made her want to know more. More about sexual attraction. About the reasons why people lost their minds in the pursuit of physical satisfaction. She understood it on a cerebral level.

She had read a great many books that depicted the acts. The feelings of lust.

And when the writing was particularly evocative she could feel those things resonating inside of her. She could imagine what it would feel like to have them for another person.

But this was different. Reckless. When those feelings were contained to a fantasy there was a safety in them.

But she was here, alone with Diego. And there was nothing to stop him from grabbing hold of her and having his way with her now.

That was the real trouble.

All those bold proclamations he'd made... Ultimately, he was right.

She did want him.

At least, she thought she did.

There was a layer of safety, of gauze between the sexual words she had read, and the experience itself. At least, she assumed so. You could read about the flavor of a peach, and get a sense for it, but it didn't truly capture the way it felt to bite into the fruit. The thickness of the skin, the texture of the pulp. The way the juice felt as it ran down your chin. You could read about all those things, and not really understand. Words didn't leave you full—they didn't change things inside of you in the same way.

She had a feeling that the physical act would be something else entirely.

But if this was the start of her independence, if this was the beginning of the life that she would create for herself, then perhaps it was exactly the right time, and Diego was exactly the right man to begin this sort of exploration with.

A man that she chose—ignoring the fact that he had kidnapped her and demanded that she sleep with him— because she wanted him, and not because her father had selected him as a worthy husband.

As justifications went, it might be a little bit thin, but she was willing to go with it. And anyway, her options were limited. That was the simple fact of the matter.

The deal that Diego was offering was infinitely better than the... Well, the other deal he was offering.

Wherein her family was disgraced, they lost all of their money, and she found herself without shelter and her father's home, and without the shelter of a husband. Because Matías would have no need to marry her if her father's business no longer mattered.

There was the matter of the inheritance, but he could find any number of women to help with that.

And Diego would simply kidnap a different one.

"You have a deal," she said, tilting her chin upward. "But there is a condition. You're not touching me until after our marriage vows are spoken."

He laughed, a dark, dangerous sound that rolled over her like a tide. "Oh, that is not too difficult a thing, *tesoro*. We are to be married in the morning."

She blinked. "How?"

"I told you. I have left nothing to chance. And really, it is morning now."

"I don't have a gown."

"But you do. I'm very solicitous like that. I took the liberty of choosing exactly what I wished to see my bride in."

"That's…creepy. Do you know that?"

"Hmm." He made a thoughtful noise. "I have kidnapped you out of your bedroom window, in spite of the fact that you were set to marry my brother. In spite of the fact that you have likely spent the past two weeks in his bed. I have been obsessed with you from the moment that I saw you and plotted a way to make you mine. Obviously I'm a bit creepy. And I've made my peace with it. Hence the kidnapping and arranged speedy marriage. Do you honestly think that pointing it out is going to shame me?"

"You're…"

"A monster? I called myself that only moments ago. Why exactly do you think that will insult me."

"A *criminal*," she said.

"I've been called worse. If you've ever a mind to find out exactly what, feel free to peruse the internet."

"I don't have access to it."

"I didn't say it would be *easy* for you to peruse the internet. I just said that you could."

"Perhaps I'm not that interested in you, Diego. If I was going to fight for internet access I would go online shopping instead of googling you."

"There is no need for you to online shop. Everything you could possibly want is already here."

"You don't know my taste."

He reached out, gripping her chin between his thumb and forefinger. "That's where you're wrong. I know everything about you. Everything. I've looked at every photograph that exists of you that's been published in public. I made a study of you every time I went to your father's house. Every item of clothing in that closet fits you. Believe me. I have made a study of your curves."

A shiver went down her spine. She should be mortified. Furious. And on some level, she was. But there was more. She felt… She didn't even know. She had never been someone's focus. Not like this. And while she knew he had other reasons for taking her, while she knew it served him in other ways, the fact remained that she did matter. He wanted her. Matías didn't want her. He didn't care. He certainly wouldn't have kidnapped her out of the bedroom window. He simply would have found another woman. Diego made it sound as if he couldn't. It was…

For a woman who had felt almost invisible for most of her life it was intoxicating in a way it should not be.

Perhaps her father had been right to protect her

all this time. Maybe her natural inclination was to be drawn to darkness.

But you have no way of turning on the light, so you might as well accept it. You might as well live in it.

She didn't see that she had another choice. Not now. Why fight when she couldn't win?

"We need to sign an agreement," she said.

"You're not really in a position to be making demands," he said, his voice dry.

"Yes," she said, "I am. I have something you want."

"By that you mean your body?"

"Yes. My body—" she tried to speak without trembling "—and my acquiescence to being your wife. I think I'm in a fantastic position to be making demands."

"By all means, list them."

"I want assurance that you will give me a settlement." She named a sum. Outrageous. She was certain that he would tell her she could jump straight off the hillside manor and into the sea.

"Double it," he said. "I'm a man of means, *tesoro*. I will hardly leave my ex-wife without access to designer clothing."

"Generous of you," she responded.

"Not at all. Of course, you should receive a healthy payment for time spent in my bed."

Heat lashed her cheeks. "Don't make it sound like that. You're not paying for…for that."

"Am I not? I find I would pay quite handsomely for access to that space between your thighs."

She gritted her teeth, well aware that he was trying to be inflammatory. Or maybe, he wasn't trying. Maybe it was simply who he was. But the man she had met at her father's house had been a damn sight more charming than the one who stood before her now. But still,

Diego, even in all his arrogance, even as he was, caused her pulse to race. And not only from anger.

"But that isn't what you're paying for," she reiterated. "You're paying for me to be your wife. That includes—" She swallowed hard. "That includes sex. It is part of being married. It's different than paying for sex."

"However you twist things so you don't feel like a whore, *querida*, it is not my concern. Twist them at will. The fact remains, that I am promising you this money."

"And I require a document."

His lips turned up into a wide grin and he reached toward the heavy oak desk that sat in the center of the room. He grabbed a piece of stationery and slid it to the center, taking hold of a gilded pen and making strong, bold lines across the paper. It made her wince, watching those thick, dark strokes of ink mar the page. As if she were watching something indelible take place before her that she now regretted bitterly, even though it was what she had asked for.

He slid the page toward her. And there it was, in black and white, the promised sum of money, her promised declaration to provide him with marital duties and an agreement to divorce when his inheritance was settled.

"This is not binding." She sniffed. "You wrote it on a piece of paper, and we have no witness."

"It will have to do, sadly. I can procure a last-minute priest, but the acquisition of a last-minute lawyer might be a bit ambitious."

"I'll keep this," she said, folding it up and holding it tightly in her hand.

"So little trust between us. Hardly a good start to a marriage."

"No, I think the kidnapping was perhaps the bad start."

"If you say so." He looked at her, his dark eyes as-sessing. "If you want something binding to seal that document, I do have a suggestion."

"What?"

That was when she found herself being hauled to-ward him, her hands pressed against that hard chest, his dark eyes cutting through her as if she were noth-ing. An insubstantial waif so easily flayed by all that raw power that he possessed.

And before she could protest, his lips were on hers.

And it was...

It was the explosion she always feared could occur inside of her. It wasn't a slow build, a gentle introduc-tion into sexuality. No. It was like being hurled into space, cast into the darkness, so black, so intense that there was nothing else. No way to see through it. No way around it.

No way through it.

His kiss was hot, vast and slick and endless and ev-erything she had ever hoped and feared a kiss could be.

Her heart was thundering hard, her entire body going weak and breathless from the onslaught of sensation that had tumbled over the top of her.

He forced her lips apart, his tongue sliding against hers savagely as he claimed her. And suddenly some-thing bubbled up inside of her, something entirely for-eign. Or perhaps, not so now.

It was the same thing that had struck her after the phone call with her father.

She had power here. She was not simply an object. He wanted her. *Diego* wanted *her*. And that made her a force of her own kind. Made her something powerful and strong. Something that he couldn't control or ma-nipulate. Or at least, not without consequence.

She returned the kiss, some unknown intuition inside of her driving her movements. She traced his outer lip with the tip of her tongue and relished the feral growl that exited his lips as she did so. He wrapped his arms around her tightly, pressing his pelvis against hers, allowing her to feel just exactly what her kiss had done to him. He was hard, long and strong and so much bigger than she had imagined a man could be.

Classical paintings had not prepared her for the aggressive outline of Diego's masculinity. Had not prepared her for the overwhelming heat and hardness, for the leashed strength.

And nothing, no erotic turn of phrase or illicitly penned fantasy, had prepared her for the desire that welled up inside of her. For the need that overtook her, wrapped itself around her throat with a decisive click, like a collar, binding her to him.

She found herself clinging to his shirt, holding on to him tightly as he continued to savage her mouth with his own.

If she had not been a hostage before, she certainly was now. Hostage to him. To pleasure. Her own weakness.

She whimpered, and as if it was the magic turn of phrase to break a spell, he pushed her away from him, taking a step back, his dark eyes blazing with black fire.

"Dios mio," he rasped, pushing his hands through his dark hair. "You are a witch."

"I'm not," she said, her voice small, her mouth bruised, her entire body buzzing with rampant heat.

"You must be." He turned, as if to go, and then he paused. When he faced her again he reached his hand out, pressing his thumb against the center of her lower lip and staring at her intently as he held it there. Then without a word he released her, walking out of the room and leaving her there alone, feeling somehow trapped and untethered at the same time.

The fact that she was unchaperoned had hit her in a particularly strange way just before he had come to kidnap her. And oddly, though she found herself in his custody now, that sense was even stronger now.

Because there was no one here to stop her from going after him. To stop her from stripping off her nightgown and climbing on top of that hard, masculine body.

She shivered. She didn't know where these thoughts were coming from. These feelings. She shouldn't have them. No, not at all. She wasn't experienced enough, first of all. And second of all... She should despise him.

She didn't.

She was terrified of him. Of what he made her feel. She was fascinated by him. By this man who was essentially a marauding modern-day pirate.

"I'm alive," she whispered into the silence of the room.

She was. She was alive and she was free.

What a strange thing, because she was also a captive. But it occurred to her then that in many ways she had never not been a captive. Captive to her father's wishes. Captive to her own desire to do whatever it took to appease her father. Then she'd been given over to Matías. And now...

She might have made a bargain with the devil, but at least it was a bargain of her choosing.

"I'm free," she said again.

And tomorrow, she would be Diego Navarro's wife.

CHAPTER FIVE

THE DAY OF the wedding dawned bright and clear. Diego hadn't slept. He had been waiting. The priest was due to show up at six to finish last-minute paperwork. Concerns regarding the church. Diego was no traditionalist, but he was a Catholic. And though he might be a bad one, there were still certain things that were nonnegotiable down deep in his soul. That everything be recognized by the church was one of them.

The divorce... He would concern himself with that later.

He imagined it would be fairly easy for Liliana to make an argument for annulment, considering coercion had been involved.

His mouth twisted into a wry smile. She had not been coerced last night when they had kissed.

He had known that there was heat between them. Heat and flame and all manner of dark desire. He had not realized it was quite so strong.

He was a man who had sampled many flavors of hedonism. A man with vast experience in the sensual pleasures of the flesh. But he had never in all his life felt anything like that kiss. A kiss.

Of all things.

It had made him shake like a green virgin.

It had also made him…jealous.

Had his brother been accessing all that passion? It made him want to kill Matías.

The world already thought him a murderer, so, he might as well have the pleasure of actually being one.

It didn't matter. Though it galled him, it didn't matter. When he was through with Liliana, he would be the only lover that she remembered, regardless of who had been there before him.

She had seemed surprised by the explosive attraction between them too. And that, at least, had been gratifying.

He wanted to own her desire.

As he would own her in only an hour.

He adjusted his cuffs and went out onto the grounds, making sure that everything was in place. It would not be a wedding ceremony anything like his first. Which had been, granted, formal at the behest of his wife, and in the confines of a church, his bride in a grand, dramatic veil and train that had taken up the entire aisle she'd walked down. No. This would be different. He had chosen a place for them that overlooked the sea, where the sun would be rising just as they spoke their vows.

And he would see all that golden light over her skin, tangled in her hair…

He closed his eyes, not bothering to question why this mattered to him at all. It was about winning. Nothing more. Winning and sexual desire. Both things he understood well enough. Anything else… He would pay it no mind.

The sooner this marriage was finalized the better. And then, Liliana was going to have to have a talk with Matías.

In the meantime, he owed his *abuelo* a phone call.

The old man answered on the first ring. "You have taken your brother's fiancée!"

He sounded delighted. "I have," Diego said. "Though I think she prefers me. Women do love a bad boy."

Sadly for Liliana, he wasn't a bad boy. He was a bad man. And the two were worlds apart.

"And I admire a man willing to stoop to such levels to win."

Winning. Was that what he was doing?

Sometimes he didn't know what drove him to do this. Except...

It wasn't fair his brother should move on to some happy life at the *rancho*. With Liliana, most of all. The very idea was like acid in his stomach.

The *rancho* had been a torture chamber when they were growing up and Diego could hardly bear to set foot on it. He would have it destroyed. Leveled to make a housing development or just left to rot. Perhaps he'd salt the earth and let nothing grow.

As for the money...

He'd gamble it away.

Finishing destroying his father's legacy while the old man rolled in his grave.

If Matías was the hero, trying to redeem all that had been dark and terrible, Diego was the villain. He just wanted it all to burn.

It was what he did. It was who he was.

A destroyer.

"I do not play to lose," Diego said. That much was true. Whether it was in a casino or in the business world, Diego had never lost.

He had a sharp mind and no morals. The two went hand in hand to create some very nice fortune, he found.

"Indeed you don't. But watch out for Matías. He may yet surprise you."

"He won't find me. And when he does? Liliana and I will be married."

"He will still have the rest of the term to find a new bride. Then the inheritance will be split," the old man reminded him.

"I have not forgotten the details of your devil's bargain, *abuelo*. No need to remind me."

"Play to win, Diego. I am rooting for you, if I'm honest."

Diego hung up, feeling that same sour stomach he'd felt when his father had looked at him with recognition, rather than hatred.

The strange thing was...

He wanted to win. He wanted everything.

And yet, he had Liliana.

His brother might find a new bride but Liliana was his.

In the moment that seemed to matter most of all.

He waited. Standing down at the bottom of the stairs, keeping watch on the time. She was late.

He would think nothing of going upstairs and dragging her back down to him if need be.

But then, he heard footsteps, the swish of fabric. He looked up, and for a strange moment felt as if he was caught between that breath before the second hand on the clock moved. Because there she was, her pale blond hair spilling loosely over her shoulders, and that gown...

It was more than he had imagined it might be. There was a spray of glittering glass beads that seemed to cling to her skin, as the fabric they were sewn into was so sheer it was as if it wasn't there. They started as a pale glisten, then built into a startling shimmer as they cascaded down. The neckline was a deep V edged in those rhinestones, and the bodice fell loose and nearly sheer, the entire gown somehow managing to conceal her body just enough, while also giving the idea that at any moment it might give way and reveal her full glory.

He had seen it and known he wanted to tear it off of her body later. And that was why he had selected it.

But just then, that was not what he wanted.

He did not want to tear it from her body. Didn't want to lower her down to the floor.

He wanted to gaze at her in that piece of art forever. Wanted to place her upon a throne and call her his queen. He wanted to worship her.

For he had never seen anything so beautiful in his entire life. Not a woman, not a sunrise, not one single thing.

She was like a ray of light floating toward him, each step she took down the stairs making the fabric swish around her legs, making it appear as if she were floating.

She was an angel.

He had brought an angel into the underworld.

If she had makeup on, it was as translucent as the gown. She looked pale, but there was a shimmer about her skin, her lips a natural pink like the first blush of a rose against the snow. She looked so young. So innocent.

He had not felt young or innocent when he had been young. Now, in his thirties, he felt nearly ancient, and as for innocence...

He had been raised by a murderer.

He had never trusted anything in the world. He had been born jaded. At least, that was how it had felt.

As if from the first moment his mother had held him

he had sensed that once she put him down his father would raise his fists to her.

And yet part of him had always craved the softness.

Because it had been there. In his life, for a moment. Just a glimmer of light in his youth that had otherwise been a horrendous log of pain.

His mother. The light shining out in all of it.

He wondered if that was why he had been so drawn to Liliana. Not because she reminded him of his mother. Not even a little. But because he sensed she had that kind of light that might cut through the kind of darkness he lived in.

But he knew how that ended.

He knew it well.

Karina had not been an innocent, and so he had imagined he might be able to hold her, at least for a while.

But there had been an innocence caught between them. Caught in the darkness of their marriage. A chance at light that had been extinguished before it had ever truly burned.

Their unborn child. Another sliver of hope, of promise, held before him and then cruelly extinguished.

He gritted his teeth, and he did his best not to think of any of it.

Not now. Not now when the most beautiful creature in all of God's creation was floating on a cloud toward him. If there was happiness to be had for a man like him, it was fleeting. And this moment might well be it.

"Happy wedding day," he said.

Her eyes met his. "Yes."

She sounded detached. Slightly dazed. But she had put on the gown, and she was here. He did not require her to be enthusiastic about it.

"Shall we?"

"Where are we…?"

"I'll show you."

He reached his hand out to hers, and this time, he had no gloves on. This time, when she took it, the soft, delicate skin of her hand met with the callused skin on his. It was like lightning, and he knew that she felt it.

She was silk. He wanted to touch her everywhere.

He voiced none of this.

He simply led her out the front door and walked her across the silent grounds. Mist clung to the grass, to the tops of the trees, and she didn't speak as they walked.

They cut through the trees and made their way to the edge of the cliff side, the ocean raging down below. The priest was already there, his expression one of utter neutrality. He had been paid to perform the ceremony. Not to have an opinion on the ceremony itself.

If he sensed that it was a strange arrangement, he did not say.

Diego looked down at Liliana's left hand then and noticed that she was still wearing his brother's ring.

He gritted his teeth but said nothing as the two of them took their positions in front of the priest.

He began to speak, delivering the standard words for the marriage ceremony. Standard vows, which Liliana spoke without meeting his gaze.

For his part, he spoke his without ever looking away.

He had done this before. Had promised this very thing to someone else.

He had kept his vows too. It was just that death had come much sooner than he had anticipated.

But the fact he'd done this before only made it more essential he keep his eyes fixed on Liliana. That he not look away. That these words be for her, and her alone.

"Do you have rings?" the priest asked.

"Yes." Another purchase he'd made before he'd actually taken his bride. He had been confident they would end up here.

He reached out and took hold of her hand, and she looked down at the ring that was there. Diego slipped it from her finger. He held it up to the light, letting both her and the priest take a long look at the glittering diamond ring that was no doubt worth a small fortune for men who did not possess the wealth he and his brother did.

Then he hurled the gem into the sea.

"I have my own rings."

He reached into his jacket pocket and produced a long velvet box. He opened it, and inside was a set of rings. Both made from a dark metal that had been twisted into ornate knots around the band. His was plain beyond that, while hers had a simple band and a second ring that was set with large, square-cut diamonds. He slipped both rings onto her finger.

Like turning the key in a lock. She was his now.

His wife.

Liliana was his wife.

Then he held the box toward her, offering her his ring.

She took it out delicately, and then with trembling fingers slipped it onto his.

He cast the box to the ground and, without waiting for instruction, pulled her into his arms and sealed their vows with a kiss that burned him all the way down.

"Your services are no longer required," Diego said to the priest, then added, "Bless you, Father."

The older man nodded, and Diego seized his bride's hand and began to lead her back toward the house.

"What was that?" she asked as he rushed her back toward the house.

"What?"

"Why? Why the rings? Why all…this? Why did we get married there? Why do I have the dress?"

"It was a wedding," he bit out. "What would you have had us do? Wear sweatpants and sit in a recliner?"

"There was no one there," she continued. "No one there but a priest. And now it's over. I don't understand what the point of all the ceremony was."

Because he'd wanted it. And he didn't know how to say that. He didn't even know how to justify it to himself. He was not in the habit of justifying things to himself. If he wanted them, he took them. He had wanted to see her dressed as a bride. He had wanted to see her in this gown. He wanted to have a ring that matched hers, so he would know even when they were apart that she belonged to him. He had wanted to say vows, real vows, not simply sign a piece of paper. He had wanted to be married in the eyes of the church, because he was Catholic enough to feel it wasn't real if that were not the case.

He did not want to think about why those things were. And he did not want to have to give reasons for them. Not to her, not to himself and not to anyone.

Particularly not now that he had agreed to a temporary term on the marriage. He just wanted. With a blinding, endless desire, and had done so since the first moment he had met her. He had thought that this might make it stop. Had thought that this might make it feel the way that he needed to.

But the need was the same. Maybe once he had her…

He stopped walking, stood with her there in the middle of the mist-covered ground. "You're mine," he said.

"For as long as it takes, you're mine." For as long as it took for his grandfather to give him his portion of the inheritance. For as long as it took for this need in him to go away. "I wanted there to be no doubt about that. I wanted you to feel like my bride. Do you?"

"If I had married Matías there would have been a party. My father would have been there. My friends. I would have chosen my dress. And then…"

"And then you would have gone back to his room, spent your wedding night with him. Is that your regret?"

She said nothing.

"You did not marry *him*," Diego continued. "You have married *me*. And this is the wedding that I wanted."

"I don't understand why you care about the wedding at all."

"Because you're mine." It was all the reason he was going to give. And he'd give it as many times as she needed to hear it.

"You're a bit crazy—do you know that?"

"Creepy. Crazy. Again, I'm not sure why you imagine I would be bothered by such things." He took her hand and began to walk again. "What I know about life, *tesoro*, is that things slip through your fingers easily. As do people. Whatever chains I can put around you to keep you with me, I will do. Never doubt that."

"Until the end," she said softly. "We agreed."

"So we did. You cannot back out now," he said. She was his. She was his. She was his. He owned her now, until the end when he sold her back to herself.

He could do exactly what he wanted with her. She had agreed. He could take her straight back into the house and rip that dress from her body as had been his original fantasy. He could. There would be no one to stop him. Least of all her. She wanted him. He knew that she did. The way that she responded to his touch, to his kiss told him everything he needed to know. Forget a wedding night, he could have a wedding morning if he so chose.

But he found he did not want it.

He had bound her to him in the deepest way possible. He had procured a priest, of all things. They were bound not just by the laws of men but by the laws of God. It did not feel like enough. No. It would not be enough until his bride begged him. Until she came to him. And then... Then he would brand her in a way that she would never forget. But he would not allow her to spin tales of how Matías would have given her a gentle and respectful wedding night. Of how she would have had a more civilized groom and a grander wedding. No. There would be no regrets. There would be no comparisons.

She would beg. He would have her beg.

"I just require one thing from you," he said.

She went stiff, and he knew exactly what she imagined he might ask for next. "You must call Matías and tell him that you've married me. That you do not wish to leave me."

He took out his cell phone and held it toward her. "That's all?"

"That's all."

"And if I tell him to come rescue me?"

"To what end?"

She looked defeated by that and took the phone. He had dialed his brother, and she put it to her ear. "Matías? I'm so glad I reached you."

He could hear the intonation of his brother's voice on the other end. Angry. "I can't say." He didn't know what she couldn't say, but her blue eyes went to his for a moment, then away again just as quickly.

"I'm not injured. I'm perfectly safe. In fact, I need for you to stop looking for me." She squared her shoulders, her posture determined. "I didn't mean to deceive you, and I never meant to hurt you in any way. But I cannot marry you because Diego is the man I really want. I left with him of my own free will. The only reason that I screamed is because he startled me. But it was always my intention to waste your time and make it difficult for you to complete your task, and then marry him. I was not kidnapped. You don't need to look for me."

His heart was pounding heavily. She didn't need to say that to his brother, and he wondered why she did. Why she was changing the story like this.

"It's okay, Matías. Truly. I regret my behavior, but there is nothing to be done. Diego and I have already married. And that means… You know what that means. All of it will be his. If you fail to marry, then all of it will be his. It's too late. We have paperwork. Everything is legally binding. We're married. It's too late."

He watched her face closely, looking for any hint of regret. But there was one thing he came to be certain about as he stood there watching as she broke the news to her former fiancé. She did not love him.

And why he should care about that he didn't know. But he did.

When she was finished, he took the phone from her.

"That was terrible," she said.

"Is he heartbroken?"

"No. Of course not. Matías is a good man but I doubt him any more capable of love than you are, to be quite honest."

"Why do you suppose that?"

"I don't know. It's a feeling I have. He treated me like a baby duckling. Like he wanted to place me in a nest safely somewhere. He did not want to love me."

"I don't see you as a baby duckling," he said. "And I do not want to place you in a nest."

No, he wanted to place her on his bed, lay her on the soft mattress and lick her from her delicate ankles all the way to her sensitive neck. He did not want to protect her. He wanted to defile her.

But he kept that to himself.

"Happy days for me," she said dryly.

"Why did you lie to him?" he asked.

She looked bleak. "I want control of what little I can get. I don't want to be a victim. I don't want to be a woman who was sold into marriage or fought over by two brothers. If it makes the news, and it will, given who my father is and who the both of you are... I'd rather be seen as a vixen." Her mouth curved upward slightly. "I'd rather be a player in the story, rather than a pawn. I am so very sick of being a pawn."

Nothing much burned his conscience. But that did.

"You have free rein of the house," he said. "You may do whatever you wish. There's a library, as we discussed last night. The grounds are yours to wander. There is no method of escape, so you can forget that."

He didn't want her falling to her death from one of the rocky cliffs in a desperate bid for too much freedom. It was difficult to gauge just how sick of being a pawn she was.

"We have a deal," she said. "Whatever I think of it. Whatever I think of you... I gave you my word."

"Yes. And I have offered you a lot of money."

"I'm not going to try to leave."

"I have some business to attend to," he said abruptly,

not releasing her hand, leading her back into the house. "I am very sorry that you do not have a grand reception. However, you will find there are some freshly made pastries in the kitchen. I shall meet you tonight for dinner."

And with that, he led them both into the house, and left her standing in the entry. He could feel those ice-blue eyes on his back as he walked away.

He knew that she had expected him to play the part of the villain. That she had expected him to be the marauder who demanded his husbandly rights.

He smiled. All the better for delaying gratification. If she wanted him to make things easier for her by taking the choice away... She would be sadly disappointed.

She would come to him of her own free will. More than that, she would be trembling with desire by the time she did.

There were few things he understood about himself right now. But this... This made sense to him.

And more than that, the very idea of her begging him...

It was a delicious temptation he had not imagined he could feel. Until Liliana, life had been distinctly boring. He felt like he'd had nothing to look forward to. And then he'd met her.

Suddenly he'd *wanted*.

Prolonging that want—this pain, this need in his gut—it was such a novelty that he found it almost enjoyable.

Of course, the truly enjoyable part would be when she was on her knees in front of him.

He was happy to wait for that moment.

CHAPTER SIX

LILIANA FELT A sense of disquiet that lingered for the entire day. She had expected him to... Well, after the wedding, she had expected him to take his *rights*. She had told him that she would sleep with him. She had expected he would see to that sooner rather than later. She certainly hadn't expected to be left to her own devices for the entire day.

Her wedding outfit had been... It had been nearly obscene. The way that the jewels and the flesh-colored netting at the top had only just covered her breasts, and the tiny pair of white panties that had been provided for her... It all seemed like she was being made into the perfect virgin sacrifice for him. Surely, he had been intending to see that underwear, or he would not have chosen it.

Her cheeks heated just thinking about it.

She had been so certain. So very certain.

But no. He hadn't demanded anything. Not at all. And why she still had those panties on, and a matching white lace bra, now beneath a rather slinky emerald green dress, she didn't know.

But perhaps he would want to *consummate* after dinner.

She shifted restlessly just thinking about it.

She had had a great many hours to wonder what that would be like. To go from trying very hard not to think about sex with Matías to thinking a bit *too* hard about sex with Diego.

The fact of the matter was she'd wondered about it from the first moment she'd met him. Before she had found out her father had planned on marrying her off to Diego's brother.

The connection she felt with him had been instant. Electric and unlike anything she'd ever felt before. So yes, she had thought about his hands. Rough and large, and she had pondered what it would feel like to have them skim over her skin. Yes, she had more than pondered it. Even now, even now that he had proved to be—whatever he was—her body responded to him. It couldn't be helped.

It also scared her.

She felt like she was waiting for a lion to come eat her.

Now she was meeting him for dinner, and she thought she might crawl out of her skin. She was going to have to sit there at the table with him and wonder... Wonder if they would be together like that in only forty-five minutes.

She licked her lips and shifted again, making her way down the stairs and heading toward the dining area.

The house was beautifully appointed, and the food was delicious. Liliana had led a privileged life. Had never wanted for beautiful things or delicious foods. But there was something different about being here with Diego. About being in this house where there was no one else, and yet somehow there seemed to be limitless freedom. She had eaten delicious, flaky pastries for breakfast and lunch, had read an extremely sensual book she'd found in the library, and had thought about doing each and every one of the things on those pages with her captor.

He was the one that made it feel like she was on the verge of something reckless. She might be under his lock and key, but the fact of the matter was as rebellions went...

Diego was going to teach her things about life, about her body, about being a woman, that no one else ever had. And that was where the sense of freedom lay. She would no longer be innocent. No longer be cosseted.

She would... She would *know*.

When she walked into the dining room, he wasn't there.

But there was a spread on the table that was like something out of a fantasy. And, as there was still no staff anywhere that she had seen, it appeared that it had been brought by magic.

There was an array of breads, thin slices of meat and cheese, crackers and fruits. Two terrines filled with soup, a large bowl full of paella and two glasses that were already full of wine. It all looked too beautiful to touch. She wandered down to the end of the table, looking over the spread. Her stomach growled, and she found that the breads from earlier were no longer substantial enough. Not as she stared down at this.

But then, there was the insistent, uncomfortable gnawing in her stomach over what might take place after the meal.

She sat quickly, taking the seat to the right of the one at the head of the table. It was natural for her to do. Her father always sat at the head of the table, and she knew well enough to know that was not her place.

A kick of rebellion hit her stomach. Why? There

was no one here. It was just herself and Diego. Why did he get the head of the table? Because he was the man? Because it was his home? If she was his wife, for no matter how long a period of time, it was her home too. Philosophically if not legally.

She stood abruptly, and then sat in the other chair, feeling bold and empowered. And not altogether the pawn she'd been feeling like earlier. Not just earlier. For weeks now.

It was just as she'd told Diego after the phone call with Matías. She was tired of feeling like she was the last person in the world that had control over her own life.

Was it so wrong to want to be the heroine of your own story? To want to have some say in what went on?

To sit at the head of the table. To control the headline.

She might be in a situation that wasn't entirely of her own making, or her own choosing, but she was going to make of it what she could.

About two minutes later, Diego walked in. He saw where she was, his dark brow corking upward. But he said nothing. He sat down to her right, easily, lifting his wineglass and taking a sip.

"Is all of this to your liking?" he asked.

Liliana lifted her own wineglass to her lips. "Yes."

"Have you started without me?"

"No," she said. "I didn't want to be rude."

The corner of his mouth curved up into a grin, one that was becoming quite familiar to her. It was wicked, slightly dark, and it appealed to something inside of her that she could scarcely understand, let alone identify. She had never thought that a smile could be indecent, but his was. At least, it licked along her skin in an indecent fashion, made her feel heat down in her stomach that was in no way rational or reasonable.

Again, she became unbearably conscious of the underwear she had on beneath her gown. Underwear that he had selected for her. In fact, she had the feeling that every article of clothing in her closet, in the drawers of her dresser had been selected by Diego himself. And she had to wonder if he had touched them. If those rough, masculine fingers had run along the delicate lace fabric.

Which made her wonder what it might feel like if those rough, callused fingers ran along the delicate lace fabric while it was still on her skin.

Her cheeks heated, and she lifted her glass to her lips again, counting on the heady flavor of the wine to distract her. Of course, alcohol might be a bad idea. As it would simply lower her inhibitions.

Fortunately, her inhibitions were very high, so it would take a great deal of lowering before it got her into any trouble.

"Did you have a good day?"

"An uneventful one," she said.

"Well, that can be good."

"Indeed. How was your business?"

"Businesslike," he responded, taking a healthy portion of meat and cheese from the platter and putting it on his small plate. He ate the food with his hands, the action sensual, sending a strange sensation skating down her spine. She opted to start on the soup. Soup was a safe food.

"Well, I suppose that can be good as well."

"Indeed." He echoed her, and much to her irritation she felt a bit of amusement at the exchange. Anger was one thing. Illicit sexual feelings another. Amusement... She did not want to feel amused with him.

"Tell me, Liliana," he said. "What was your favorite thing to do at your father's house?"

"You already know," she said. "Read."

"Did you read today?"

That made her face get warm again, due to what she had read earlier. "Yes."

"That's good. I'm gratified to know you're not needlessly punishing yourself by lying around doing nothing but wearing a hair shirt."

"Martyrdom has never suited me."

"Really? Because you seem like a fantastic candidate for martyrdom."

"Why do you think that?"

"Well. You were willing to marry a man of your father's choosing in spite of the fact you didn't love him."

She frowned, reaching out and taking a piece of bread off the platter at the center of the table, peering into it fiercely. "Is that what you think?"

"Yes."

"I have a sense of obligation to those I love," she returned. "If that's martyrdom…"

"It is. Essentially."

"I don't see it that way. It's just that I'm not selfish. You don't…" She took another bite of bread. "You don't understand."

"Make me understand. Here we are, at our first meal together as man and wife. Make me understand you, Liliana."

"Will you make me understand you?"

"I'm creepy and crazy," he returned dryly. "Can you truly understand either of those things?"

"My mother died giving birth to me," she said, seeing no point in stringing him along. In giving him the satisfaction of toying with her as a cat did a mouse. "My father lost my mother right as I came into the world. He lost her because I exist. Tell me, how can I do anything to try and please him?" She blinked. "I... I wanted to please him, that is. For that reason. Not because I'm a martyr. But all of this has led me to the conclusion that my life really has never been mine. It's a frightening thing, Diego, to realize that you have never truly been free until the moment you were kidnapped from your intended path."

He picked up a piece of bread and dunked it in olive oil, taking a bite and making a musing sound. "Never truly free until you were in my arms? Is that what you're saying?"

"No," she said. "And yes, I'm in a cage after a fashion here, but it's a different one. And... I don't know. I don't know the right answer. That's the problem. I've wanted to please my father all this time, but... Part of me knows that it isn't fair for him to hold my mother's death over my head. Not that he blames me directly, but he definitely uses it. Has used it to keep me in line. To make me into the daughter that he wanted me to be."

"And he's a bastard for doing it," Diego said. "Though, in my experience fathers tend to be bastards."

"Your father..."

"We are not talking about my father." His words were hard, definitive. "Continue to talk about yours. About you."

"Obviously, I never knew my mother," she said. "My father's all I had. I don't think of myself as a martyr, primarily for that reason. It's just... He's all I have."

"You have me now," he said.

The air between them thickened. She... He meant it. Whatever it meant to him, she didn't know, but the words he'd spoken had been spoken with absolute conviction. She had him. And there was no tart response for that. Not when he had spoken with such sincerity. With such gravity.

She had him.

He had her—that much was true. He had kidnapped her out of a window.

But those simple words he had just spoken gave her power as well.

"And very good bread," she said, not sure what else to say. "Who is… Who is making our food?"

"I've hired some people on the mainland to supply us with meals. It's being brought over in a helicopter by one of my men that I trust implicitly. No one else knows where we are."

"I don't know where we are," she said.

"That isn't going to change. While I understand our agreement does benefit you, you must understand that our trust is somewhat limited."

"Well. I understand why my trust toward you would be."

As soon as she spoke those words she felt guilty. He had been…

She thought of the way he had taken her hand today. Of him throwing that ring into the ocean. Giving her his rings. The way he had looked at her the first time he had seen her in the wedding gown. None of it was normal. But it was…

Somehow, she had the feeling that Diego had stronger feelings for her than anyone else ever had.

"Thank you," she said. "For dinner. For… Oddly, for rescuing me from your brother."

He lifted a brow. "I thought Matías was a good man?"

"He is. But a future with him is not actually what I wanted. Having options… Which our deal has provided for me… I don't even know what I'll do with that kind of freedom. I've never had money of my own. I've never done anything but exactly what my father asked me to do. And I felt obligated to do it. But this… It's like you gave me permission to find another way. Somehow, taking away my choice gave me a world of choices I didn't know I had."

"Are you thanking me for kidnapping you?"

"Not in so many words."

"Well, I'll take whatever I can get. Even if it's not in so many words."

"What business do you do?" she asked. "That isn't gambling."

They spent the rest of the meal talking about his various investments and endeavors. He grew animated when he talked about the different restaurants and clubs he had been involved in. His mind was fascinating, filled with creative solutions to all manner of problems. Ways to get attention that she doubted anyone else would think of, methods of erasing formerly bad reputations, the process by which he managed to take an unknown location and turn it into the hottest destination for anyone with money and cachet.

She imagined that it was that darker side of his nature, the one that saw kidnapping her as a viable solution to his present problem, that made him such a brilliant businessman. He wasn't bound by societal restrictions. Wasn't bound by law, or really anything.

He didn't have to work hard to think outside of the box, because he had never been in one.

She, in contrast, had spent her entire life in a little box. One that she had stepped in and stayed in of her own free will. Being around a man like Diego was electric. She wondered then if that was part of their instant connection. Or at least, the connection she felt on her end. That fascination.

After they were through with dinner, there was hot chocolate and churros, and by the end of that, Liliana felt almost content. Warm and sleepy. Something in her wanted to move closer to Diego. Curl up against him like a cat. She couldn't figure that out.

She didn't feel entirely motivated to figure it out.

He would ask now. For their wedding night. They just had their wedding feast, after all. And they had talked. Gotten to know each other better. She hadn't anticipated that being part of any of this. But she wasn't sad about it. Not at all.

She felt happy.

Like this moment between them had nourished a deficit in her soul she hadn't even known was there.

"Are you finished, *tesoro*?"

Treasure. He called her his treasure, and sometimes she felt like he meant it.

The entire scene from their wedding played itself back in her mind again.

Yes. Sometimes, she felt like he meant it.

"Yes," she said, nerves quivering in her belly.

"Good. I imagine it's time to retire. We've both had a very long day."

"Yes," she agreed.

He stood from his chair, then reached down to help her up as well. She took his offered hand, electricity zipping from her fingertips down the rest of her body.

He lifted her hand to his lips, brushed them over her knuckles. "Good night," he said softly. Then he lifted his head, straightened and walked out of the room, leaving her standing there. Alone.

He didn't possibly mean to… He wasn't…

And she certainly couldn't be disappointed if he were. She was a prisoner. She had agreed to the physical aspect of a marriage under sufferance.

Immediate heat rolled over her. Not just because she was lying—to herself, in a bald and blatant fashion— but because just thinking of being with him made her feel hot with longing.

She went to her room, stripped her dress off and left it on the floor. Then she crawled beneath the blankets, restless and edgy. Sure he would come to her. Any moment. Any moment.

She lay there in the dark, nothing between her bare skin and the sumptuous comforter she was resting beneath, and that insubstantial underwear selected by Diego himself.

Every time she shifted beneath it, it stimulated her. Made her nipples feel sensitive. Made her breasts feel heavy. And that place between her thighs felt hollow.

She would be ashamed of her own weakness except...

He had said this would be part of the relationship. He had gotten her thinking about it. And now he wasn't here. It wasn't fair.

He was supposed to take the mystery out of all of this. He was finally supposed to be the one who...

It was just about sex. Not him.

She was twenty-one years old. It was past time she knew what all the fuss was about.

She flopped around like a discontented fish beneath the blankets for at least an hour. And then, it became abundantly clear he had no intention of coming to her room.

What game was he playing? And what was she supposed to do about it?

Suddenly, she felt hot. She pushed the blankets off her body and curled into a ball when the cold air hit her.

She felt goose bumps break out over her skin, and still, inside she was burning up.

She shoved the blankets down toward the bottom of the bed, pushing her feet beneath them, and finding that uncomfortable as well. She tried the reverse, shoving the covers up, and placing them over the upper half of her body while leaving the lower half exposed. Still, she was restless. Another hour had passed with her shunting the bedding down from one end of her mattress to the other, and sleep still eluded her.

She was well past the point of being jet-lagged. She'd been in Spain for nearly three weeks. It was him. Him.

He was the one who had gotten her to agree to this wretched devil's bargain. And now he wasn't even calling in his end of it.

He was keeping her in suspense on purpose. Torturing her.

It was two years of torture. That's what it was.

She growled and rocketed up out of bed, pacing the length of her bedroom. She could go into the library and read. And that was what she decided on. But after an hour of that and two sentences read, she gave up.

And she found herself walking down the hall, barely conscious of the fact that she was still only wearing that white underwear.

She hadn't been to his room before, she realized, but somehow, she was walking as if she would find it easily in this maze of rooms. But she sensed somehow that he wouldn't have placed her too far from him, and she was gratified to find she was correct when she pushed open the door just on the other side of her library door, and found it looked inhabited.

There was a large bed back in the darkness, and she could only just make out the shape of him.

"What exactly are you playing at?" she asked, the veil of darkness provided by the room covering her near nudity and making her feel bold.

"Liliana?"

She felt like a virgin sacrifice standing on the edge of the Dragon's cave. She could hear him beckoning from the darkness. And she was just stupid enough that she was going right toward it.

"No. It's your other wife."

"I wasn't expecting you. You went to bed hours ago."

"So did you. And you're still awake."

"True."

"What game are you playing?"

"I'm not playing any game. I'm sleeping. Or rather, I was attempting to."

"You know what I mean," she said.

"No," he said. "I find that I don't. Perhaps you would care to elaborate?"

"We agreed. We agreed that physically this would be a real marriage. And this is our wedding night... And you..." She huffed out a breath. "Stop torturing me. You have me on edge. Waiting for the moment that you're going to... Just take it."

"I told you," he said, his voice like dark silk, "I have no intention of taking anything from you. I intend for you to give it to me. Enthusiastically. I intend for us to give to each other."

"I don't... I don't understand. You said you wanted sex. And I agreed to give it to you."

"What sorts of sex have you had, Liliana? Because the fact that you seem to view this as a commodity that you hold, for you to take or give, mystifies me. Sex is meant to be shared between two people."

Her blood was pounding so hard in her face, her cheeks throbbed. "I don't... I... If we're going to do it, I don't see why we can't just do it now."

She heard the sound of his bedclothes rustling, heard footsteps as he began to walk toward her. "I asked you a question. Is my brother such a selfish lover that your view on sex is that it's a chore?"

"I'm a virgin," she said, ignoring the thick shame that wrapped itself around her throat and made it nearly impossible to breathe. She hadn't meant to announce it like that. She hadn't meant to announce it at all. It wasn't his business. It wasn't anyone's. She hadn't wanted to make herself so vulnerable.

But she felt vulnerable. The very fact that she had gone in here to confront him about leaving her alone on their wedding night proved that.

Because it wasn't the anticipation that had driven her. It was the fact that it had...hurt her feelings.

Good heavens. She was wounded over the fact that her kidnapper seemed to be able to resist her.

He might be crazy, but she wasn't much better. Clearly.

She heard his footsteps and saw the dark outline of his form as he moved nearer to her. "A virgin?"

He was big. So much bigger than she held him in her memory. It made her feel very, very small. He could break her with one hand. Destroy her.

She sensed he could also make her feel things she'd only ever dreamed of.

It made her tremble. There had been spare few unknown things in her life. She'd been protected by her father, her husband selected for her. And this...

This was very, very unknown.

"That's what I said." She sniffed, keeping her posture rigid, trying not to shrink back from embarrassment or anything else.

"That's very interesting. And especially interesting you didn't see fit to let me know until now."

"I didn't see that it mattered."

"And yet, you think it does now?"

"I wanted you to understand why it feels...unfair. It's not like I have a lot of experience. It's the unknown. I don't know what to expect. As far as sex goes. I'm just... I was just lying in bed, waiting for you to come. And I don't even know what exactly I'm waiting for. Can't you understand how that frays one's nerves?"

"First of all," he said, his tone almost gentle, "you're not waiting for an execution. If all goes well, you're waiting for an orgasm. Perhaps several of them. And that shouldn't terrify you."

"Orgasms don't terrify me," she said, grateful that the light wasn't on. Grateful he couldn't see how furiously she was no doubt blushing. "But the idea of..."

"Penetration?"

Her mouth flew open, then snapped back shut. She couldn't speak.

"Yes," he said. "That, I think, is what worries you."

Yes. It did. But, it was more than that. And she didn't want to have this conversation with him. Didn't want to talk about it at all. Because she couldn't put into words exactly what scared her. Beyond the element of the unknown and the physical pain. It was the fact that they were going to be so... So close. Skin to skin.

And of course, now she was standing there in his room wearing nothing but her underwear. At least it was dark. But still. What had she been thinking? She should have put on a robe. Or that green dress. Her wedding gown. Something.

"I'm turning on a light," he said.

"No," she protested, her voice an impotent squeak as he flicked a lamp on.

He was standing there wearing nothing but a pair of tight black briefs and she forgot for a moment to be embarrassed, because she was too busy taking in the sight of him. His chest was broad, covered with dark hair that tapered down to a thin line as it bisected his well-defined abs. His hips were narrow, his thighs muscular, and it made her curious what exactly he did to acquire such a physique. But she imagined that wasn't polite conversation. Of course, they were both in their underwear. So polite conversation might very well be out the window.

She was embarrassed, for a moment, when she realized she had been standing there staring. But only for a moment. Because then she realized that he had been staring right back. That he was looking over her body. And she forgot to be embarrassed at all, because he looked...hungry. For her.

And yet again, she tried to remember if she had ever felt like anyone particularly cared about her. Matías certainly hadn't cared whether or not *she* was his wife, or some equally suitable woman. Sometimes she wondered if it mattered much to her father who she was as a daughter. Or if any child willing to do his bidding would have done. He didn't know her, after all. Not really. He only knew who she tried to be for his benefit.

Diego seemed to care.

That heat and black fire in his eyes told her it was something more than caring too. Something dangerous and illicit that she had never imagined she would ever inspire in a man. She hardly knew anything. Had barely been kissed. Why would a man want her that way? She didn't have bombshell curves, or dramatic beauty. Whenever she made the style section of the papers they praised her slim figure, it was true, but the kind of figure that clothes hung off had little to do with the kind of figure men found sexually desirable.

Except, Diego seemed to desire her.

But he hadn't come to her. It didn't make sense. Particularly not with how he looked at her now.

"Beautiful," he said.

"Then why didn't you come for me?"

"I meant what I said to you before. I was not going to force myself on you."

"We had an agreement," she said weakly.

"That is not why a man wants a woman to come to his bed, *tesoro*. Not because there is an agreement. Not even because we spoke about it. I want you in my bed because you desire me. You're here now because you are…curious, I think. But curiosity is not enough either."

"What do you want from me?"

"I want you to need it," he said.

She blinked. "I don't even know what that means."

"Then you don't need it yet."

He turned away from her, and she was stunned for a moment by the sight of his sculpted back, her throat going dry. And then, indignation took over. "Are you rejecting me?"

"Does it bother you?"

"Yes," she said.

He turned again. "Why?" His tone was savage, intense.

"Because I… Because I…"

"What?"

"I want you." The words spilled out of her mouth, and she was too upset to be embarrassed by them.

"Do you?"

"Yes," she said.

"Does your body ache for me?"

"Yes," she said, her voice low and steady. "Does it make you happy to hear that?"

"Yes," he said, his voice transforming into a purr. "It is what I want to hear. But I must know more. When you were lying in that bed were your nipples tight?"

She flushed. "Yes."

"And between your legs… Did you ache for me, my darling?"

Shamefully, even as he spoke the words, she felt it happening to her. As if it were by magic. As if he were magic. A dark, dangerous kind of magic that she should want to run from.

Except, she had already made the choice to run to him. And fleeing now seemed silly. Especially when he had tried to turn away and she had stopped him.

She tilted her head up, did her best to stand there before him, proud and unashamed, even while her knees shook and her stomach pitched. "Yes."

"We can start with that," he said, closing the distance between them, grabbing her chin between his thumb and forefinger. "You want me. From there, I can teach you need."

Before she could speak, he claimed her mouth with his, and her entire world bloomed into color, and she found herself being dragged against his hard body, found herself surrendering to his touch, his kiss. To every slick pass of his tongue against hers.

This wasn't about what she should want. Wasn't

about what she should do. It wasn't about being good. It wasn't about anyone but her.

And she realized then, that it was about taking. Because she felt claimed already. But he was also doing something to her, giving her something that she had never imagined she needed.

Need.

He angled his head, parting her lips, taking the kiss impossibly deep. And the shaft of near pain that seated itself between her thighs made her understand that word in a way she never had before. *Need.*

This was need.

She expected fear to come and overtake that need, but it didn't. There was nothing. Nothing beyond the slick glide of his tongue against hers, those large, warm hands skating over her curves. His body was hard, crisp chest hair rough, where she was smooth. Where she was soft.

She had known that reading about things like this with a layer of fantasy between herself and the words couldn't compare. But she hadn't fully appreciated just how overwhelmingly tactile making love to a man would be. It was everything. Overwhelming all of her senses, his musky, male scent intoxicating her, making her feel dizzy and bold and like a stranger inside her overly sensitized skin.

But she liked it.

"I had such fantasies," he said, his voice rough. He slid his hands down to her rear, cupping her and lifting her, urging her legs around his back as he carried them to the bed, lifting her and setting her so that she was standing on the mattress and he was still rooted to the floor. "Fantasies of tearing that wedding gown off of you earlier, throwing you down on the floor and making love to you there. Did you know?"

"No," she said. "I didn't. Because you didn't do any of that. You didn't do anything at all."

"No. Because something changed."

"What?" She nearly whispered the question. She was desperate to know what had changed since the moment he had stolen her out of her bedroom window. What had changed between them. What had changed in his heart, in his soul.

"I don't know," he said, looking up at her, his dark eyes filled with a wildness that she couldn't quite guess at. "All I know is suddenly I wanted to lift you up. To put you up above me. I wish to gaze at you, just like this. To worship you." He reached up, grabbing hold of the clasp on her bra and making quick work of it, dragging the insubstantial lace down and away from her body. Before she fully took on board the fact that she was topless in front of him, he was already dragging her panties down her thighs. He was eye level with... With her.

And then, he was moving, his large hands holding her steady as he pressed his mouth to the heart of her, tasting her deeply, his tongue sliding through her folds, the blunt tips of his fingers digging deep into her hips. She began to tremble, began to shake. She forgot to be shocked. Forgot to protest. Her entire world was focused on this moment. This man. So powerful, so ruthless. Ruthless enough to pull her out of her bedroom window at midnight, to steal his brother's fiancée. To force her into a hasty marriage.

And yet, he was down below her, that dark head bent as he lavished her with pleasure. As he licked and sucked and kissed that most intimate part of her. Her thighs trembled, her knees turning to water, her entire body beginning to unravel beneath that expert mouth. And still, he kept on. Still, he ravished her.

She clung to his shoulders, her fingernails digging into his skin as pleasure crested over her like a wave, her orgasm out of her control and she was like a wholly new creation because of it.

Giving control of her body, her pleasure, to another person was...

Then, he looked up at her, and their eyes collided, and she felt something twist in her chest, shifting, turning on its side. She had the strangest suspicion that it might never right itself. That she might never be the same again.

He looked... Like a fallen angel. That wicked mouth was curved into a grin, that wicked mouth that she now knew could do indecent, obscene and delicious things. It had been so intimate, and yet, she wasn't ashamed.

She found herself kneeling, her knees pressing into the mattress. And she leaned forward, kissing his lips, tasting her own desire there, the evidence of what had just happened between them. He growled, wrapping his arms around her and holding her, not so tightly as he typically did when their mouths met, but like she was a fragile thing that he was afraid he might break.

Then, she found herself being pushed backward, that large, muscular body looming over her as he gazed down. He kissed her neck, on down to her breast, sucking her nipple deep into his mouth, then tracing a circle around it with his tongue before turning his attention to the other. She became lost in a world of sensation. An erotic dance of Diego's making. She could make no more comparisons between reality and fiction, because she could make no more comparisons at all. She could hardly form a thought. She could only feel.

By necessity she had been a cerebral creature for most of her life. Someone who observed life with a healthy dose of distance between the ivory tower her father had placed her in and the world around her.

But there was no distance here. It was raw and intense. Skin against skin, mingled breath and pounding heartbeats that tangled together. His tongue against hers, his fingers in her hair. His sweat-slicked chest rasping against her breasts as he held her close, as they kissed.

And somehow, by her own hands or his, she didn't know, his underwear was gone, and she could feel the blazing hot length of him against her hip as they continued to kiss, as he pressed his hand between her thighs and tested her readiness with his fingers. First one, then another. She gasped slightly at the unfamiliar intrusion, but that gasp gave way to a moan as he slipped his thumb over that sensitized nub between her legs, as he drew a response from deep inside her body, echoes of the climax she'd had only moments before.

He removed his hand then, settling between her legs, murmuring something in Spanish against her lips. "I don't…"

She had been about to tell him that she didn't speak Spanish, but her breath caught in her throat when he pressed against the entrance to her body. He murmured something else, but she couldn't understand. And then he was filling her, the pain blinding. She gritted her teeth, battling the urge to push him away. She wished, badly, that she could recapture the pleasure she'd found in him only a few moments before.

But then he was inside of her. He was breathing hard, his breath hot against her neck, and she became dimly aware of the fact that she was hanging on to his shoulders like a cat trying to claw its way far from danger. She forced herself to relax, to grow accustomed to the sensation of him being inside of her.

"I'm sorry," he said. "I told you it might hurt."

She was about to tell him that he had not told her that, except she realized it had been buried in that broken Spanish she hadn't understood. She would tell him later that she didn't speak Spanish. An absurd thought to have when a man was inside of you, probably.

Then he was kissing her again, and things began to feel a bit more pleasant. He shifted, sliding his hand down beneath her lower back, skimming over her bottom, down to her thigh as he lifted her leg, urging it around him as he withdrew slightly, then thrust back home.

It didn't hurt that time. It felt...

By the time he did it again it almost felt good.

And then, he began to make magic inside of her yet again. That same, sensual veil that had been wrapped around them before was suddenly there again as she got lost in his kiss, the way his hands moved over her body, and that slick, deep glide of him inside of her. She felt full, but it was good now. Felt invaded, but she welcomed it. This was what it meant to be possessed. To be desired. If she could have taken him deeper, she would have. She would have taken more. Taken everything.

She clung to him, lifting her hips in time with each thrust, chasing the building release inside of her. In the end, it wasn't even that delicious friction inside of her that did it. In the end, it was him. He began to shake, lowering his head, his movements becoming wild, his face buried in her neck. The sound that rumbled in his chest was feral, came from deep inside of him. He froze above her, looking as though he were in the most intense, wretched pain. And he looked at her. Those dark eyes unveiled for a moment. And in them she saw...

She didn't even know what it was. A depth. A need. All she knew was that it called to her. That it reached inside of her and seemed to find a matching piece she hadn't known was there. She clung to him as he shuddered out his release, and her own caught hold, dragging her right down with him.

They clung to each other in the aftermath, like shipwreck victims in the middle of the sea, storm tossed and broken. But together.

He tried to move away from her, but she held on to him. She didn't know why. Didn't know why she wasn't showing a little bit more self-preservation. Why she wanted to hold on to him when really, it was the last thing she should want. But she didn't know who he was. Not anymore. Any more than she knew who she was. Something had changed inside of her and she didn't know if it would ever be right again. She didn't know if she wanted it to be.

The outside world... Well, out there they made no sense. He was her kidnapper. More than ten years older. She was an overprotected heiress who shouldn't exist outside of books or the nineteenth century. Individually, they were difficult enough, and together they were impossible. But somehow, on this island, secluded in this bedroom away from the rest of the world, it all seemed right.

She couldn't explain why. Not if pressed. Not at all.

She only knew that it was.

And she wanted to prolong this moment, this one of peace and rightness, for as long as she possibly could.

Finally, he rolled away, dragging her with him, bringing her half on top of his body. She laid her head against his chest, against his raging heartbeat.

"I will get condoms," he said.

She felt a slight pang at the realization they hadn't used protection. But it wasn't followed by any sense of panic. Which she couldn't quite understand.

Her mother had died giving birth. And while she'd always expected to have children of her own, she had always felt connected to the danger of it. Even in the modern era.

But she'd made her peace with her desire to have children versus any potential danger years ago. And that wasn't what she expected to scare her now.

It was the fact she would be linked to Diego forever.

She waited for the fear.

It didn't come.

She suspected she might be linked to him forever already.

"Okay," she said.

"It won't take long."

"I'm surprised you didn't have them here already. Considering you took care of every other detail."

"I intended to bring you here to make you my wife in a permanent sense," he said, his voice betraying no hint that such a thing might be strange. "But, now things have changed. I suppose precaution should be taken."

"Of course," she said softly.

She didn't want to think through what he'd said too deeply. So instead, she pushed it aside. And she clung to him. Marveling at how she felt. Altered. Changed. Closer to this man than she had ever felt to another human being.

"Diego," she said. "Why did you want a wife?"

"My inheritance."

"No. That's why you needed to get married. Why did you want a wife…?"

"I'm Catholic," he responded simply.

"Still. I would imagine you could make whatever deal you needed to make... From a religious standpoint... That it would be legal and not recognized by the church."

"I imagine. But, I have never much seen the point in marriage if it wasn't forever."

"Do you...? Do you believe in love, Diego?"

She was afraid of his answer. Very much. Because she feared that she might believe in love, and she feared even more deeply that she might be falling into it with the last man on earth she should.

"Yes," he said. "I believe in love."

For a moment, relief washed over her. Then he continued.

"I believe there are soft, brilliant people in the world with a capacity for love that the rest of us don't deserve. I believe in the power of love to heal, to change. But I also know that love can be twisted and turned, used as a weapon. That there are people who can never be reached with it. People who are beyond it. Love is a powerful force, but there are enemies it cannot defeat."

"So you believe in love, but don't believe that everyone can...feel it?"

"Yes."

"Why?"

"I've seen it," he said. "It's not a secret..." He cleared his throat. "It is not a secret that my father murdered my mother, *tesoro*."

"What?"

"My father is a murderer."

CHAPTER SEVEN

DIEGO HAD NO idea why he was telling her this. Especially after what they had just shared. He should make it about pleasure. About spending the night exploring her beautiful body. He could be more careful the next time they made love. Could withdraw before he climaxed. Though, part of him rebelled at the idea. Still, when the subject of birth control had come up Liliana did not seem as horrified as he had imagined she might.

But they were not making love again. They were talking about his father instead.

"Tell me," she said.

"My mother was a wonderful woman. I think we should start there. She was my introduction into the idea that there was good in the world. Believe me when I tell you there was little evidence of that elsewhere in my house. My brother and I were terrified of our father. He was a tyrant. If he had one emotion in his body beyond selfishness and rage, I would be surprised. He was like a black hole. Consuming and destroying everything in his path. And so, we did our very best to stay out of his path. Matías, he tried to be a good son. And for a while I did too. But then our mother had an accident. She was out riding and she... She fell from her horse. That was the story."

He paused, looking away from Liliana. From her impossibly beautiful, innocent face that was so shocked to hear such a story. It was his reality. His childhood. He had never been shocked by it. He had been broken the day he'd found out his mother was dead. Had cried the last tears he had in him. Even as a man, when he had endured hideous loss, he hadn't been able to weep. He had expended every last tear back then. But he had not been surprised.

What must it be like to not immediately assume the worst of people? She would. After this. After him. He had kidnapped her, for heaven's sake. Had brought her here. Was holding her... Well, it wasn't exactly against her will, not now. But... She would learn. She would learn at his hand. And this story would be part of it.

"She didn't fall from her horse?"

"She did. But my father was in pursuit of her. He shot her. I do not believe that it killed her. But the horse was spooked and threw her. Her official cause of death was a broken neck."

"Diego..."

"My father told me all of this in a drunken rage only two days later. I was eleven years old. And after that... After that I didn't care, Liliana. I did not care if he killed me. I tempted it. I welcomed it. I found my matching darkness and I let it bleed free. He had a shop with classic cars inside. I lit it on fire."

She was staring at him still, her blue eyes round.

"And I laughed as everything he cared about burned."

You must learn to let go of things when they're broken, Father.

He remembered saying those words back to the older man, defiant and filled with his own murderous rage.

"I really did think he would kill me that day," Diego

continued. "He beat me within an inch of it. But then, he laughed. He laughed, because he said he knew my anger. He said if I would only feed it, I would become just like him. Matías... He did not understand him. But me... I'm a chip off the block."

"You aren't," she said ferociously.

"No. It's true." He would not go into Karina. He would not speak of her at all. It didn't matter. Not now. Not now that this marriage was temporary. "And I did not tell you this story in order for you to talk me out of my vision of myself. But you asked what I think of love. Love is why my mother married my father. A misguided sense of love is why she stayed with him. And love is what killed her. It did not change him. It did not shine a light on his dark places. Instead, his darkness consumed her. They say that love redeems people, but there are those who are past redemption."

"Didn't you say you were Catholic? Shouldn't you believe that too?"

"I'm into Catholicism mainly for the guilt."

"Don't you think you deserve something other than guilt?"

"No," he said. "In fact, I cling to the guilt. That might be the one thing that separates me from my father. The fact that I have the capacity to feel it. Even if it is difficult."

"Do you feel guilty for kidnapping me?"

A strange bleakness flooded him. "No," he said honestly. "And that is a concern."

"But, here we are."

"Yes. Because whatever I feel, it's not strong enough to make me want to give you back. You're mine, *tesoro*."

"Yes. You continually remind me of that."

"Does it bother you? Do I scare you?"

She shook her head. "No. But you have to realize… If I'm yours… I believe that makes you mine." She kissed him then. He should stop her. He should yell at her and ask her if she had heard the story at all. Tell her not to speak to him again of love. To not kiss him so tenderly when he was trying to make sure she understood that he was a monster.

But he didn't.

He simply let her kiss him.

Let her drag them both to the edge of that place where nothing existed beyond pleasure and need. Where there was no him and no her. No light or dark. Just a brilliant blending of the two.

She had just asked him if he would let himself have something other than guilt.

Well, he would let himself have her.

So he did. All night.

CHAPTER EIGHT

Two weeks in Diego's house. Two weeks in his arms. Two weeks in his bed. Liliana hardly knew who she was, and she was all right with it. In fact, she liked this new version of herself better than the old her anyway. She laughed easier, for one. She felt bold.

The night before, at dinner, she had sat on his lap during the meal and fed him meat and cheese with her hands. Then, he had licked her fingers, put her up on the table and licked her everywhere else.

He was strange, her man. Complicated and, yes, filled with darkness. But there was something else too. He needed. He needed her to touch him. Periodically, during the day, she could sense restlessness falling over him, and when she placed her hand on him, she could almost instantly feel that unsettled energy leaving his body.

It always made her think of the boy he had been. The boy who had lit his father's shop filled with cars on fire. The boy who hadn't known another way to let his anger escape. The boy who had lost his mother. His softness. His reference point for love.

Diego believed in love because to not believe in it would be a dishonor to his mother's memory. She understood that.

Just as she understood he thought that he was like his father.

Thought that there was something inside of him that meant love was not for him.

She wanted—more than anything—to change that.

She only wished she knew how.

So she touched him whenever she could. Held him at night while he slept. She was his, and she made sure that he knew he was hers.

Today he had been particularly moody, and she wasn't sure why.

She was sitting in the library reading a book when he stormed in. He had that look on his face like he might throw her down and ravish her, and she was more than ready. But then he stopped, his posture rigid. "Pack a bag."

"Why?"

"We are going back to Spain."

"Why are we going back to Spain?" He wasn't getting rid of her, was he? Was their time together already at an end? That was impossible. Two weeks would not be enough time for his grandfather to be convinced of the legitimacy of their relationship. It couldn't be over. Not now.

Suddenly, the idea of having money, having a life that was full of things and freedom, but lacking in Diego, seemed desperately sad. And not like something she wanted at all.

"We have a wedding to attend," he said.

"We do?"

"Matías is getting married." He looked blank when he said it. "It was in the paper. She's the daughter of some famous…horseman, I guess."

"Oh."

"Does that bother you?" The question was asked with an almost-savage intensity.

"Why would it bother me? I'm married to you."

"Temporarily."

The word was like an ice pick straight through the center of her chest. "Yes. I suppose that's true."

"I thought perhaps it might bother you to see your ex-fiancé married to another."

"You know for a fact that he was never my lover," she said. "That I did not have any sort of real relationship with him."

"Does it bother you to attend his wedding?"

"No. Unless you're planning on leaving me there in Spain without you."

He looked completely taken aback by that. "Why would I do that?"

"You're acting very strange."

"Because I…"

It occurred to her then, the implications of the marriage. Of course if Matías was able to marry it meant that Diego would not get the total sum of the inheritance. They'd be sharing it. Considering Diego had stolen her from Matías in part to prevent that, he couldn't be very happy.

"Are you upset about the money?"

He looked genuinely confused. "What?"

"The money. Now you'll have to share it with Matías."

"Right. I suppose so. But I will get what's coming to me as well. I don't need any of it."

"Do you hate your brother?" She had to wonder if he did, with the way he was going after him like this, the way he'd tried to sabotage his chance at his inheritance.

"No. I don't understand him, not any more than he understands me."

"Then why does this matter?"

He made a sound that would have been a laugh if there were any humor in it. "My father tortured us. He took our mother from us. Now my *abuelo* is playing games with the only compensation we have for being sired by a madman. I don't like my life to be under the control of anyone else. I don't like being manipulated."

"But you allowed it," she said. "You married me."

"I won," he bit out.

"Then what's bothering you?" He said nothing. "You're still afraid that I'm going to run away from you, Diego. Is that it?"

"What has happened here has not felt real," he ground out.

Those words echoed that deep feeling inside of her. That somehow, secluded on this island, the two of them were a fortress. A fortress that could never be destroyed, but once exposed to the outside world, to the elements...

She had no confidence in it there.

In the ability of a sheltered, recently deflowered heiress to hold on to the attention of a man as complicated and interesting as Diego. That was the problem. She imagined that, mostly, to him she was a novelty. And novelty didn't last.

"What happened here has been as real as anything else in my life," she said softly. "At least... At least it was of my choosing."

"Was it?" he asked. "I kidnapped you. I brought you here. I certainly didn't ask for your permission."

"No. You didn't. But I gave myself to you of my own free will, and I have most certainly given myself to you of my own free will since. Can you doubt that the last couple of weeks were anything other than my choice?"

"That," he said, his voice hard, "is sex."

"Fine. So it's sex. Very good sex, I might add. That doesn't mean it isn't real. It doesn't mean I didn't choose it."

"It doesn't mean it was wise of you."

She put her hand on his face. "Was it wise of you to kidnap me?"

His dark eyes stayed trained on hers, and he turned his head, kissing her palm. "Of all the things I've done, kidnapping you was perhaps the wisest."

"Let's go to the wedding," she said. "I'm more than happy to attend as your wife."

The moment he set foot on the dry, cracked ground of the *rancho*, Diego's stomach twisted. He had not felt this way when he had returned to procure Liliana. Possibly because he had been distracted by the idea of claiming her as his own—which he had done repeatedly in the days since—but now... Now he felt consumed by the memories. This place. Which contained so many wonderful, terrible things.

The hacienda had not changed, not the red roof and wrought iron details. Nor had the grounds, arid and wild with the only real green the lawn stretching out before the house. The rest was all tangled vines and olive trees, washed pale in the midday heat.

He'd have thought that if he were to gain half ownership of the *rancho* he might burn the place to the ground. As he had already started to do years ago.

But for some reason, now that thought forced him to imagine what Liliana would think of such a thing. Needless destruction.

"Do you like this place?" he asked as the two of them walked to where the grounds had been set up for the wedding. Chairs positioned toward a flowered archway. He vastly preferred the ceremony he and Liliana had shared.

"Yes," she returned.

"You think it's beautiful?"

"Why?"

She stopped walking and looked at him, her blue eyes far too keen.

"Because if you like it then I should not allow anything to happen to it."

"Why would anything...?"

"If I have ownership of the place it would be my inclination to not let it stand."

"Because of your father?"

"Yes."

"To continue to destroy his dream."

She knew him so well. Understood him. She had that gentle way about her, soft and searching, and far more than he deserved. "Yes," he confirmed, his voice rough. "I might as well burn it all to ash, no?"

"Is this where...?" She cleared her throat. "Is it where your mother was killed."

"On these very grounds, yes. You can see the appeal of destroying it."

"Matías loves this place," she said. "I didn't spend a lot of time getting to know him. I often felt like he was more a guardian than anything else. We didn't have deep conversations. But he told me a great deal about the *rancho*. And he... He is consumed with it. It's everything to him. I'm not sure that he has much passion in his entire soul, but what is there... It's for this place. If you destroyed it, you would be destroying his dreams. Not your father's."

Something inside him twisted. "You forget, I kidnapped his bride. You think that the fact he cares about this place might deter me from doing something to it?"

"You wanted me," she said, her hand on his arm. "That's different. If you want the *rancho*...you should have your part of it. But if you want to ruin it... You didn't take me to destroy me."

There was something about her touch. It always made him feel calm. Made him feel something that was otherwise often beyond his reach. And it made him want more. Futilely.

"That doesn't mean it won't be the end result."

"You said you didn't hate him," she said, quietly.

He didn't think he did. But sometimes...sometimes it felt a lot like envy.

That Matías seemed whole.

When he'd seen the headlines of the upcoming wedding and the story of it being a love match, he'd nearly choked on that envy. Why should his brother be able to love? After everything they'd been through, Diego could not. That Matías seemed to find it wasn't just. But then he'd realized who the fiancée was.

Camilla Alvarez. The daughter of the recently deceased Caesar Alvarez. Matías had purchased the entirety of the older man's estate, and to Diego's mind, it all seemed a bit convenient for the two of them to suddenly find love.

He intended to look into that at some point over the course of the day.

Neither of them spoke as they continued to walk into the venue. They were ushered to their seats, and Diego stood again, driven by something. He didn't know what. Some need to get his footing back. Because God knew Liliana had made him feel like he was slipping.

He was so possessive of her he could hardly think straight most of the time. Work held no appeal. Truly, nothing did. He wanted to hold her close. Keep her forever. He had gotten condoms, as he had promised he would, and he had used them. But he would be lying if he said part of him didn't wish that the first time they were together had resulted in a pregnancy. Because he did not want to give her up. He wanted to keep her forever, as impossible as that was.

For so many reasons.

Even if they had not made the deal, by now he would have come to the conclusion that at the end of all this, once his half of the inheritance was his, he would have to let her go.

He already knew what became of things he cared for.

Already knew that he left nothing but destruction in his wake.

He would not tempt those feelings again. Not with Liliana.

He was the dark one. The bad one. Diego Navarro, beyond redemption. Everyone knew it. The people here certainly did. He had felt the judgmental eyes of everyone in the place from the moment they had come in, and Liliana was oblivious to it. Because Liliana had no idea.

His father was a murderer. And everyone here thought he was one as well.

He was the villain.

It was high time he reminded himself of that.

"I'll return in a moment. Do not disappear, Liliana. Remember, I can destroy your father with a phone call."

She said nothing to that, the brightness of shock in her blue eyes making his gut twist. The threat had been unnecessary and he knew it. But he'd still felt compelled to issue it. To remind her, not of what he held over her head.

But of who he was.

He left Liliana sitting in her chair, and walked toward the hacienda, his mouth set into a grim line. When he opened the door, it was not his brother he saw standing in the antechamber, as he had expected. It was a woman, standing with her back to him. The woman he had seen in a picture with Matías only a week or so ago. She had very short hair, and she was beautiful, much like a little dark-haired pixie.

"Well," he said, drawing on all his experience playing the bad guy to make sure he sounded just like one. "Don't you make a radiant bride."

She whirled around, her dark eyes wide, her expression full of all the fear that hadn't been in Liliana's eyes when he'd taken her from her room that night. This woman knew what he was.

"Diego, I presume," she said.

"You make this sound very like an overdramatic soap opera," he drawled, moving closer to her. "I must say, I am impressed with my brother's resourcefulness. Often, his scruples prevent him from claiming certain victories. I myself have never understood why he'd limit himself the way he does."

"I'm not entirely sure what you're talking about," she said. "Matías is my lover. He has been. Liliana's defection was only a good thing for us."

She was a good liar, was the little pixie. And Diego had to wonder if the part about the two of them being lovers was true enough. Though, Diego doubted they had been before. Matías was far too good to plan to marry Liliana while keeping a woman on the side.

"It is a very nice story," he said. "But I already read

it in the paper. You know, my brother fancies himself a good man, but he is not so different from me. He simply draws lines around moral dilemmas as he sees fit. And I have never seen the point of doing so. He decides that certain actions are *right*, and certain actions are *wrong*. He has decided that his motivation for inheriting the *rancho* is higher than mine, and therefore, he must win at this game. I require no motivation myself beyond my need to win. To be satisfied. I don't need to pretend I am being *good*."

"Is that why you took Liliana?"

She was spirited, this woman. He admired it.

"She was simply a means to an end." As he spoke the words, he thought of their weeks together. And again of her coming down the stairs in that dress. The tightness in his chest. His heart. The darkness in his soul that cried out for her light. "Like everything else."

"Did she go with you of her own free will? Or did you kidnap her?"

"Oh, I kidnapped her." Images of her in his bed, in his arms, flashed through his mind. And that drove him on. A reminder of who he was. A reminder of what this was. "But, she was convinced quickly enough to marry me. I just had to have her throw out that lie to Matías so he wouldn't come searching for her. He's not very trusting. He believed so quickly that she would betray him. It's a character flaw, for sure. If I were you, I would watch out for that later on. If he were to walk in now, I imagine he would have a lot of follow-up questions for you. Particularly if he were to walk in when you were in my embrace."

Diego took another step toward her, and the woman took a step away. "Don't come anywhere near me," she said. "You're a villain."

She had no idea. Truly, no idea. "To you. But a villain is his own hero. I read that somewhere once. I quite like it. Although, I am not overly concerned with being either. I'm simply concerned with winning."

"Well, Matías and I are getting married today. So you're not going to win."

"Am I not? Because I will get my share of the family fortune, if I choose to press the issue with my lawyer, I will probably end up with a stake in my brother's company." He didn't care. He wondered if he ever had. Or if he was still a small boy lighting things on fire because he didn't know what else to do with his rage. "And he has had to settle for second best when it comes to wives. Yes, I think my victory, while not total, was handily done enough."

The door to the house opened again, and a small woman in a black dress walked in, casting him a severe look. "It is time," she said.

"I had better go take my place in the audience, then," he said. "But rest assured and remember this. My brother might talk about being good, he might talk about doing the right thing, and in the end he might do the right thing by you, whatever that means. If it looks like a permanent marriage, or an attempt at commitment. But he will not love you. That is something the men in our family are incapable of."

He walked back out into the brilliant sunlight, repeating his own words back to himself as he took his seat next to Liliana, who looked at him and smiled as if he were the stars, and not simply the dark night sky.

He was not capable of love. And neither was Matías.

He couldn't be.

If after all they'd been through, Matías could find love, while Diego lived in the darkness…

He would be alone in it.

Sitting out there in the midday sun, surrounded by people, with Liliana's hand on his arm, he felt more alone than he ever had.

And the truly startling thing was, he found it un-bearable.

CHAPTER NINE

THE WEDDING HAD been beautiful, and Liliana was not at all surprised to discover that she wasn't envious in the least. Not of the spectacle. Not of the groom. And not of the gorgeous reception that followed. The bride and groom were scarce during the event, but there were a lot of people eating and reveling, and she was ready to do the same.

The venue was made into something so beautiful. It was hard to believe such a place could have such a dark past. But Matías had worked very hard to turn it into something else. Something new. White lights strung over a clearing surrounded by olive trees, a stage with a band playing off to the side. There was an elaborate canopy with cakes and other sweets set beneath it that looked incredibly tempting after a long day in the sun.

It was so wonderful to be here, and she couldn't quite explain why. Except she felt free and happy.

Except… Diego was like a storm cloud at her side.

Diego, who could not see a way to redeem this place. Diego, who only saw the darkness.

"I'm going to go get cake," she said, touching his face, trying to see if she could conjure up some of that magic between them now. It didn't seem to be working. She shifted, dragging her fingertips along the line of his jaw, down to his chin, rubbing his lower lip with her thumb. A spark ignited in those dark eyes, and he looked at her.

"Would you like cake?" she pressed.

She doubted even sweets could improve his mood, as dark as it was, but she would do her best.

"What I would like is us to return to our hotel room in Barcelona," he said, his words filled with meaning.

She knew exactly what he wanted to do in that hotel room. It was the way he felt most comfortable connecting with her, and it was most definitely the best way for him to break one of his moods.

Not that she didn't like it. She did. But just for a while she wanted to be here with him. Out in public and on his arm. Wasn't that reasonable enough?

"Yes," she said. "And we will." Her body felt warm just thinking about it. "But, I would also like cake."

"Far be it from me to stand in the way of you and your sweets. By all means, *tesoro*, go and get yourself some cake."

She didn't want to leave him, not now. Not when he was in such a strange space. He hadn't said anything but she could feel it. Being here was hurting him. She wanted desperately to fix that.

"Will you dance with me first?" she asked.

He looked at her, his expression unreadable. "You want to dance with me?"

"Yes. I don't know how to dance, though," she said. "You'll have to teach me. Like you've taught me to do… other things."

Her words seemed to propel him forward, and he took her into his arms, holding her close as he led her to the dance floor.

His hold was firm and sure as he wrapped his arms

around her and led her in time to the music coming from the band on the stage. He spun her in a circle beneath the lights, a blur of glitter above her head. She felt like she was flying. And when she landed, she was safe in his arms.

When he drew her back to his chest, she pressed her hand over his heart. It was racing, like it always did when they made love.

Like just touching was an echo of that intimacy. She carried it with her—there was no denying it. It made her feel linked to him in a way she'd never felt linked to another person. Ever. Not by friendship, not by blood.

It was the same for him. She knew it was.

The song ended and she could sense that people were staring at them. He released his hold on her, and she slowly let go of him, looking around with a growing sense of disquiet.

Several of the older villagers were giving Diego exceedingly hard glares, and then moving to her with looks of pity. She couldn't fathom why anyone would pity her. She was with the most beautiful man here. She stared right back, hoping her expression said exactly that as she allowed Diego to lead her back to a table.

"Get your cake, *querida*," he said, his eyes focused somewhere past her.

She nodded and moved away from him, feeling strange to be so far from his side after weeks of isolation with him.

She had felt that way when he had gone off to wherever he'd gone before the wedding ceremony. She wondered what he'd been up to. If he had gone to see his brother. And if so… What words had the two men exchanged? Diego was in such a strange headspace, she had no idea exactly what his goal was for being here.

To show his grandfather that he was married, perhaps. To prove that she was real.

Maybe he had gone out searching for his grandfather. But she hadn't seen a man she thought could be Matías and Diego's grandfather anywhere in attendance anyway.

She chewed her lip as she wandered over to the cake table.

"Señora Navarro."

Liliana looked toward the sound of her name and saw a small woman dressed in black, a severe expression on her face. Maria. The housekeeper. She had gotten to know her over the course of her stay with Matías.

"Hello, Maria," she said.

Maria shook her head. "I cannot believe you married *him*."

"I… I'm sorry for any pain I might have caused Matías," she said. "I am. But Diego…"

"He's a murderer," Maria said. "I doubt your darling new husband has confessed that to you."

The air rushed from Liliana's lungs, leaving her dizzy. "He is not," she said, feeling rage sparking her blood. How dare she say such a thing about Diego? He had been a victim of his father's horrific darkness when he had been a boy. And to tar him with the same brush…

"He is," the older woman insisted.

"How dare you say such a thing about my husband," Liliana said, her voice trembling. "This is his home as much as Matías's and he should not be insulted here."

"He killed his first wife," Maria continued, ignoring Liliana's tirade. "Everyone here knows it. I hope that you are entertaining him in his bed, or you will likely meet the same fate."

A *wife*? Diego had never mentioned having a wife before.

They say worse things about me.

Feel free to peruse the internet.

Those words came back, echoing in her mind. It didn't matter what this woman thought. She knew Diego. She knew that wasn't true.

"Do you know where he was before the wedding? He was menacing the bride just before she prepared to walk down the aisle. He mentioned you, of course. He says you're a means to an end. If his end is money, then perhaps you are safe. But if there is something else that he has his mind set on, then if I were you I should be concerned. He is a very bad man. A *diablito* from the beginning. The staff who have been here from the beginning have all said this. Matías is good. He has defied all expectation, everything his father taught him, and he is a good man. He is like his mother. Diego is his father. He is the devil. He was then—he is now. And everyone in this village knows it. They all remember. They know that he is responsible for the death of Karina Navarro as certain as his father is responsible for the death of Elizabeth Navarro. Ask him. *Ask him* and see what your husband tells you. But perhaps make sure there are witnesses when you do."

Liliana's head was spinning. She felt dizzy. She felt ill. She couldn't imagine Diego harming anyone, least of all a woman. Which seemed insane considering that he had kidnapped her, but she knew him. She knew him intimately. Had felt his body move inside hers more times now than she could count. She cared for him. She cared so very much. And she could not imagine that she might have come to care for a murderer. Or a man who saw her simply as a means to an end.

But why had he gone to talk to Camilla, Matías's wife? What had he been thinking doing that? What was the point?

She didn't want cake. She wanted answers. And she had a feeling she wasn't going to get them easily.

Her husband wasn't a devil. At least, she didn't think he was. But he was a brick wall.

She walked across the dark garden area, beneath the string of lights that hung like a glittering web overhead. And she went to find her husband. "I want to go," she said.

His dark eyes flashed. "Why the sudden change of heart?"

"We need to talk."

One corner of his mouth tipped up into a rueful smile. "I see. Perhaps one of the villagers has come to set you straight about the manner of man you married?"

"Something like that."

"We can talk here." He spread his hands wide.

"No. We're not going to talk here. We're not going to make a scene."

"Why not? I live for a spectacle."

"I don't," she said. "I don't, Diego. And this is *our* marriage. *Our* business. I will not trot it out for all the world to gawk at." Their relationship was private and special. It wasn't about what other people saw or thought. At least, it hadn't been on the island. That had mattered to her. As a woman who had been raised to care more about appearances than anything else, that they'd built a relationship in the dark, with only each other as witnesses, meant more than just about anything.

"That is the entire point of us attending the wedding today, *tesoro*," he said. "To cause a spectacle."

Of course. He had wanted to come to his brother's

wedding with the woman who would have been the bride. And Liliana had been foolish enough to not realize that. She had let go of Matías completely and utterly. Simple for her, since she'd never truly cared about him.

Their marriage was about two people: Liliana and Diego.

It was so strong inside of her that she had imagined it had to be the same for him.

She was a fool.

"Yes. Perhaps for you it was about creating a spectacle," she choked out. "But not for me. I wanted to attend a wedding with my husband."

"We do not have a real marriage," he said softly. "And that is because of you."

"Nevertheless. Whatever our marriage, however long it lasts, is our business. It was just you and me on the island, Diego. Just you and me." No past. No Matías. No Camilla. No angry housemaids intent on spoiling the fantasy that Liliana had built up of her husband.

She had *known*. While she had been there, something in her had known. The moment the rest of the world was invited into their union, it would introduce ugly, hard reality. Reality she did not want to cope with. Oh, as silly as it seemed, she preferred the fantasy.

"Then we will go," he said, his voice hard. She didn't know why he had decided to agree. Maybe what Maria had said was true. Maybe he was, after all, a stone-cold murderer intent on destroying her the moment they were in private. But she didn't believe that. Not really. Her sense of self-preservation was strong enough that if she felt that were true on any level she would not go off with him. But she didn't believe it. Not really.

He took her arm, and the two of them walked away from the revelry, waiting until Diego's impossibly ostentatious sports car was delivered to them. He got into the driver's seat, and the engine roared as he sped toward the roadway. And she had to wonder if he intended to kill them both with the way he was driving.

"Don't worry," he said. "I've done a bit of racing in my day."

"Not on a public road, I should think." She sniffed.

"All kinds of places." He laughed. "You are truly so sheltered, Liliana. You have no idea what kind of man I am. Or maybe you do, and you don't want to know."

Those words stung. Because they were true.

She wanted him to be all that she imagined him to be.

She wanted him to be the fantasy husband she'd created in her head.

Tonight was the first night she had been afraid—truly afraid—that he might not be. That she might be deluded by sex and a charming, dark voice that had made her fantasies a sweet and dirty reality all night long in his bed.

She had been so sure she was smarter than that. So sure that she wasn't enough of an idealist to buy into it.

She had trusted herself. Her feelings.

The low-slung car hugged each and every curve of the road as they made their way down into the city, all brightly lit as people began to emerge from their homes to take part in the celebrated nightlife of Barcelona.

They pulled up to the front of the hotel they were staying in, and Diego turned the keys over to the valet.

They walked up the vast front steps and into the ornate building, and Liliana barely had a chance to enjoy the gilded marble lobby with its rich, velvet furnishings, because Diego was whisking her to the elevator that took them to the penthouse. They hadn't stopped to look at the room earlier. Rather, Diego had simply brought their things and had the staff handle them. She didn't have time to enjoy it now. Because when the door shut firmly behind them, Diego rounded on her, his dark eyes blazing with black fire. "Go ahead. Make your accusations."

"What accusations do you expect me to make?" He knew. He knew because…

There were only two options. He either knew because he'd heard them as rumor… Or because it was true.

"I'm not playing a game with you, Liliana. Tell me what you think of me now, wife? Tell me what manner of man you were told you married."

"My first question is, why did you go off to play the villain with Camilla? What did that serve? Why harass Matías's bride?"

"I *am* the villain," he said, his tone dark. "It would be disappointing if I didn't make an appearance in the last act to menace, wouldn't it? It's just bad storytelling."

"Why? Why are you obsessed with the idea that everyone see you that way?"

"I wanted to see what this marriage was. If he'd found a woman to fall in love with him." His words were dripping with disdain. With hatred.

"And are you satisfied with your answers?"

He looked shocked by that line of questioning. "It would seem to me," he said, his voice dark, "that there is a certain amount of injustice in the fact that my brother could escape the life we lived being who he is. Finding love. Finding marriage. Living on the *rancho*, redeeming it."

"Why isn't that fair?"

"I can redeem nothing. I can only play in the darkness that my father instilled inside of me. Matías is our mother. He is…he is made of different materials. And I have never understood *why*. I've never understood how that was fair."

"Life isn't fair, Diego, or did you miss the class they gave on that?"

He made a scoffing sound and turned away from her, pacing the length of the room like a caged tiger. "Such a rich thing to be lectured on from a cosseted rich girl."

"My mother died giving birth to me," she said. "I never knew her. I never had the chance. She never even got to hold her child. Tell me how that's fair, Diego? My father didn't take the opportunity to then become two parents in one. To love me enough to cover my loss. No, he saw it as an opportunity to manipulate me into doing his bidding. Tell me again about fairness."

"I tried. I tried to overcome my past. I tried to love. It ends in nothing. It ends in darkness."

Disquiet filled her. She remembered the words Maria had spit at her.

He's a murderer.

Like his father.

"What happened, Diego? Tell me." She would rather know. She would rather know and face whatever demon came with the truth.

"You are not my first wife."

Those words felt like a punch to the stomach. She didn't want them to be true. She didn't want what Maria had told her to be true. But now, looking at him, at the horrible bleakness etched into his handsome features, she worried that it was.

"You never mentioned you'd been married before," she said.

"I don't like to talk about Karina. But the people in the village where I'm from have little else they like to talk about. The beautiful, vivacious woman that I married when we were both far too young." He shook his head. "They think they *know*. They think that it was the same as my father, and sometimes I wonder... I *wanted* to be in love, Liliana. I wanted to believe that I could escape what I was. I'd spent years losing myself in debauchery, trying to forget. Thinking that if I divorced myself from any and all connection I could at least keep those around me safe. And hell, in the process I might kill myself. And then the world really would be safe."

He was rambling, a string of words that ran together in a dark endless river. And none of it was answering the most important question she had.

"Did you kill her?" she asked.

"Yes."

CHAPTER TEN

THE WORLD FELT like it was tilting and she had to grab the back of the couch in order to keep from falling down. "Diego... I don't... I can't..." It made no sense. He wasn't a good man, her husband, but she couldn't imagine him killing anyone apart from his father. She had no trouble imagining he would happily put an end to the man who had made his life so miserable and stolen his mother from him.

But a woman? His own wife?

She couldn't believe it. She wanted to run away from this. Wanted to hide. But she had to face this. And him.

She wasn't a little girl locked in her father's house anymore. She was a woman. Her own woman.

"Diego," she said, her voice so much stronger than she had expected it to be. "Did you kill your wife?"

"Not with my hands," he said, his voice rough. "But the fact of the matter is, she ran off with a man who was worse than a coward, and she found him preferable to me."

Relief washed through her, and perhaps it shouldn't have. But he hadn't killed her. Not really. And that was all that mattered to Liliana. "Start at the beginning."

"It is not a pleasant story, and you won't like the outcome. The most that I can say is that what I love, or what I strive to love, tends to meet tragic ends."

"Diego…"

"I married her. I cared for her. She is dead," he said, his voice flat. "Does the rest matter?"

"Yes," she said, "it matters to me. Because you matter to me. And I want to know…"

"We were married for two years," he said. "Only two. I was twenty-five. She was twenty-seven. We met at a club, and we were both intoxicated. Not with each other, mind you, but with a substance of some kind. It was instant lust. She was wild and possibly the only person I had ever met who was more untamed than I was. How could I be anything but fascinated by that? I thought… I thought that would be the way. My mother had been sweet. She had loved my father in spite of all that he was. And I imagine that if I found a woman who was my equal in debauchery that then perhaps it would all work. But our marriage was never anything but toxic. Fighting, and then…"

"Sex," Liliana said, jealousy prickling over her skin. She was angry with herself. Angry for being jealous of a dead woman. A woman who clearly hadn't had the happiest of relationships with Diego.

But still. She'd been with him. Touched his body. Been brought to ecstasy by him.

No other man had ever touched her. It didn't seem fair.

"A year and a half into the marriage she became pregnant."

That word truly was like a slug to the stomach. Another woman. Pregnant with his baby. It burned her up inside.

"I had never wanted children," he said, "but I was… happy. Though Karina and I had our differences I thought we would have incentive to make our marriage work because of the child. I was happy to have a child."

"But you don't…"

"No. I don't have one. Because when Karina was about six months pregnant she informed me that she was leaving me for another man. My wife. My pregnant wife had found someone else. Someone infinitely preferable to me and my moods."

"What happened?" she asked, keeping her tone gentle.

"This is why people imagine I killed her. But the truth of the matter is it was nothing so nefarious as a car accident. It was just that… She was the only one in the car. And she was in the passenger seat."

"How?"

"She was with *him*. And he is alive and well, though he will not tell his version of the story. The truth is he was high and he ran their car into a cliff. The side that Karina was on. And he left her there. He escaped the car, leaving his pregnant mistress to die slowly. Leaving *my child* to die slowly inside of her. Karina was not innocent—that much is true. But she didn't deserve that. My child was innocent, Liliana. The only innocent in that entire tangled web. It can't be escaped. This darkness in me. It doesn't matter what I do. If I touch it, it dies. I might as well be a murderer."

"How? How can you possibly come to that conclusion?"

"She preferred the sort of man who would leave her in a car to die over me."

"I hate to speak ill of the dead," Liliana said, "but your wife sounds like an idiot of the highest order. Her bad decisions have nothing to do with you."

"And yet she's gone. And my child…"

"I'm sorry," she said. "I'm sorry about your child. And I'm even more sorry that everyone blames you because of your father."

"They blame me because they know that I must have been a truly terrible husband, whether she died by my hand or leaving me, it doesn't matter. The evidence of what I am remains. I might as well be a murderer."

"No," she said. "You're not a murderer."

"A kidnapper. A villain. A blackmailer."

"You have been gentle with me. You knew that I liked books. You talked to me. You have shown me pleasure. You've given me pleasure before you've taken your own every time we've been together. You have asked me more questions about myself than any person I've ever known. Do villains do that, Diego?"

"You are different. You always have been. You... You are the thing that I fear most, Liliana. And yet, I still couldn't stay away from you. That tells you everything that you need to know about me."

She frowned. "You are afraid of me?"

"You are that rare piece of light. You remind me of my mother in that sense. Make of that what you will."

He was trying to make it sound sordid in some way. Trying to take what they had and reduce it. She wasn't going to let him. "Say what you mean, Diego. Stop making menacing, leading comments. You might as well tie me to the train tracks if you're going to be this much of a cliché."

"Why I was drawn to you," he said. "You remind me of what it's like to have a light shine in the darkness. But I also know what happens in the end. The light is consumed. And I know what I am."

"I know what I am," she said. "And what I am is much stronger than I thought it was. I'm not just a creature created to atone for someone else's death. I'm not a weak-willed socialite. I am not your kidnapped victim. I'm not Liliana Hart. I'm Liliana Navarro and I am not afraid of you."

"You should be," he said, his voice rough. "I consume all that I touch. I destroy beauty. I break delicate things."

"No. That's giving yourself way too much power. You're an angry boy who has never learned to let go of the pain in his past. But that doesn't make you damaged beyond repair. You think that you were born a certain way and there's nothing you can do about it. You think that Matías was magically gifted with something that you can never have. That isn't true. It's not. You have a choice, and you can make it."

"A choice to do what?" he asked, his tone dripping with disdain. "What choices do I have in my life? The choice to keep you prisoner for the rest of forever? The choice to date until I fall in love and settle down in a suburb somewhere and have children with my lovely wife? What choices? I learned what men are capable of when I was a boy. I have seen the very worst end to a relationship that exists. I hate my father. And I hate even more the fact that he looked at me and saw not only his blood, but a soul he seemed to understand. I have tried to overcome it. And I will not try again."

"But you wanted to stay married to me."

"I wanted to *own* you, Liliana. I never wanted to *love* you."

His words fell flat over the top of all the pain already roiling around inside of her. They didn't surprise her. Not at all. He was so very committed to this. To this idea that he could not overcome what he was. And again, she saw, with a startling clarity, exactly why. Exactly what he was doing.

He was protecting himself. He had always done that.

From the time he was a boy he'd had to. He had endured hideous loss, and the loss of his wife... Of his child... He talked about it now with a kind of defiance, a certainty that it was the darkness in him that had caused it, but she recognized it as the same kind of blame she had taken on herself for her mother's death all her life.

She had always known that she wasn't truly the cause of her mother's death. But there was a comfort in taking on the mantle of that blame. It gave her a purpose. And most of all, it gave her protection. It allowed her to hold herself separate from the world around her. In her case, it had allowed her to justify the fact that she let her father tell her what to do. And by giving her father that kind of power she took away all responsibility for herself. She didn't take risks. She didn't make choices. She read books. She observed life rather than participating in it.

And because of that, she never had to risk anything.

Diego was doing much the same, but he didn't have a father to tell him what to do. He simply had one who had given him a monster's blood. And he could blame that monster for anything. For everything. And it kept him from ever loving and losing someone again. Yes, she could see him.

That angry, scared little boy who wanted to burn everything down. It was what he still did.

He was afraid. Afraid of being hurt. Afraid of loss.

But he wanted her. And that was the thing. He hadn't been able to stop himself from taking her. And whatever justification he was using for that now, she could see the truth. He was caught between wanting to protect himself, protect her and keep her locked away on his island.

Whether it made sense or not, her touch did calm him. She made him... Maybe *happy* wasn't the word.

She didn't know if she had ever seen Diego truly happy. But he was settled within himself when they were naked, lying in bed together. More at peace with the demons in his soul than he was otherwise.

If she could make him happy, it would be the most amazing thing.

She was strong. And he was good. And those were the two things he did not seem to be able to believe. He was afraid he would break her. But she would not be broken. Moreover, while he might possess the strength to destroy her, he never would. She trusted that. She doubted her father had spent one moment worrying about the darkness in him. Doubted he had ever ago-nized over the ways in which he had harmed his wife. Yet Diego took on the guilt of every sin committed not only by that man, but by his wife's paramour. That was not the act of a bad man.

He had sparked something in her from the moment they had first met. It had been like finding another piece of herself. She couldn't explain why. How some-thing could be so strong and instantaneous with no evi-dence behind it. But since then, it had proved only to be the truth. He was a man separated from the world by his own fear. A man who had experienced everything, while she had experienced very little. But that com-mon bond of loss, of wrapping themselves in a shield so strong and tight the world could never touch them, remained. "You're *my* light," she said. "Don't you un-derstand that?"

"No," he said.

"It's true. I was just drifting along in the gray. Maybe it wasn't the blackest night like you've experienced, but it was a haze. I didn't know who I was or what I wanted. And you gave me this… This chance at freedom that I had never once imagined for myself. You shone a light on all these hidden places inside me. You made me understand passion. You are not darkness, Diego. Not in my world."

"You understand nothing."

"I understand everything that I need to. Diego…"

"Don't talk," he said. "Not anymore. Do not forget who it is you're dealing with."

"A man who wants to watch the world burn so that it will all go away and he can be safe from it?"

"If you insist on keeping your mouth so busy, perhaps you could do it in a fashion that I might find more pleasurable."

She found herself being pushed to her knees in front of him, and she realized what he was doing. The exact same thing he had been doing earlier when he had gone to seek out Camilla before the wedding.

He was trying to put her in her place. And put himself in his. That preferred role of villain, rather than a man who seemed as if he no longer knew who he was or where he fit into the world.

Lost. He was lost. Beneath all that certainty, all of his hardness, he was a man so desperately lost and alone who needed someone to take his hand.

But if he couldn't accept that yet, then perhaps she could reach him by taking hold of another part of him.

She knew that he expected her to get angry. That he expected her to fight back.

She refused. She would show him just how strong she was.

She lowered her head, her hair falling into her face. Then she looked up, reaching her hands toward his belt and undoing it slowly, then moving to the rest, making quick work of the button and zipper, drawing them partway down his hips before reaching inside his underwear and curving her fingers around his hardened length, drawing him out toward her.

"How could you think this would be anything but my pleasure?" she asked just before she closed her lips around him. He was intoxicating. Masculine and beautiful, and essentially Diego. The man who had become her entire world so very quickly. He forked his fingers through her hair, and pulled at her for a moment, as if he was trying to get her to stop. But she knew the moment that he gave up, surrendered, guiding her head rather than trying to pull her away. A rough groan escaped his lips, and she took pleasure, pride, in the fact that she was reducing this man to nothing. He thought he was so very strong.

He thought that he could break her.

But she was going to break him. Utterly. Completely. He was hers.

She lifted her head, meeting his gaze, glorying in the tortured expression etched across his handsome face. "You're mine," she said, her tone hard, possessive. Every bit of her meaning it, as deeply and truly as he had all the times he'd said it to her. And he had. From the beginning. This was beyond both of them. That he thought he could turn away from it, that he thought he could scare her away was laughable.

The only thing that scared her was a life without him in it.

He was her opposite in so many ways. Dark and dangerous. Jaded. Experienced. And yet…they were the same.

In their souls, they were the same.

She angled her head, dragging her tongue along the

length of him, a feminine satisfaction rolling through her when she felt him shake, tremble.

She took him in deep, and she put every bit of her motion into it. There was so much. So much that she wanted him to understand. About himself. About her. About the two of them together.

She could stay on her knees like this in front of him forever, pleasuring him, making him feel good, and it wouldn't be a sacrifice. Because every ounce of his pleasure echoed inside of her. Didn't he know? Didn't he understand?

Everything that he felt she was, he was for her.

She wrapped her hand around the base, stroking him as she continued to pleasure him with her mouth, as he began to lose hold of his control, his grip tightening in her hair as his hold on the world went slack.

It was back to that feeling. That there was just the two of them and nothing else mattered. She wished she could hold on to it forever. Even though she knew it wasn't possible. The world would always be out there. The opinions on Diego's past. The temptations and distractions that came with everyday life.

But here, in the bedroom, with nothing between them, they could get back to this. Back to each other. Back to themselves.

She was never more her than when she was naked with Diego inside of her.

He growled, hauling her to her feet. "Enough. I need you. All of you."

"And you can have me. All of me." Slowly, ever so slowly, she began to remove the dress that she was wearing. It was red, a much-bolder color than she usually favored, as typically, something so rich and intense washed out her already-pale features even more. But there had been something about this gown that had set Diego's eyes alight, and she had wanted to hang on to that. Had wanted to pursue it. And now, she pushed the delicate straps down her arms, lowering the zip slowly. Grateful she had decided to forgo wearing a bra, only a pair of matching red lace panties remaining as she let the dress slide into a silken pool at her feet.

He looked hungry, and she wanted to be the thing that filled that need.

It was deeper than sex. She knew it. She wondered if he did. There was a hunger in his soul, the thing that responded when she placed her hands on him.

They had both been lonely for so long. So very, very lonely.

It was his turn now to drop to his knees, wrenching her panties down and parting her legs. She wobbled slightly on her high heels, and he gripped her tightly, clinging to her bottom as he pleasured her the way he had done that first night they'd been together. As he worshipped her, drawing her pleasure tight inside of her like a bowstring, making her feel as if he might snap her in half.

She didn't know how long it went on. She simply lost herself in it. Not just the physical pleasure, but the intense, spiritual connection that came with it. That sense of her soul being wound around another person's. They weren't alone. They were together. Every intimate act, so deep and personal, would have been shocking to her if it had been with anyone else. But with him it was communion. With him, it was a deep exploration that went beyond bodies. It was necessary. The fulfillment of this aching emptiness she hadn't fully realized had existed in her before her eyes met Diego's across a crowded room at her father's house.

He flicked his tongue cleverly, his fingers plunging deep inside of her, and that string broke. She gasped, clinging to him as she rode out her release, as he continued to eat into her while her pleasure pulsed on and on.

He was everything. *This* was everything.

And she knew without a shadow of a doubt what it was.

He believed in love. That some could give it, and some could never properly receive it. She knew that he thought it wasn't for him. But it was. Because the love inside of her heart had been created just for this man in front of her. She had never believed in soul mates. A woman who was convinced of the fact that her father was going to select her husband could not afford to be sentimental about such things. But she believed in him. And he had changed everything she had imagined to be possible. He was her soul mate. It didn't matter if it was a cliché. Not when it was true.

There was no other man she could love. And that meant there was no other man built to receive that love.

It occurred to her then that no matter what he called it, no matter what he felt in return, it would always feel like enough. Because giving him her love was what she was made for. Worshipping his body, being with him. Being the one whose touch calmed him… It fulfilled something in her.

Whatever he gave back would be enough. She would love if it could be everything. But the fact of the matter was, she knew that whatever it was, it would be everything he had to give. And because she had been made for him, it would be enough.

She bit her lip, trying to decide if her next move was the wisest one. Ultimately deciding she didn't care at all. "I love you," she said.

That fire in his dark eyes turned sharp, his expression going molten. "What?"

"I love you, Diego. I love you so much." She dropped to her knees, so she was on the same level as him, and she kissed his lips, tasting him deeply, tasting the intimacy they had just shared on his mouth. "I love you."

"No," he said fiercely. "No." He grabbed hold of her wrists and hauled them both to their feet. "Don't say that again."

"I love you," she said.

"Don't be like my mother," he said, the words tortured. "Don't love me."

"You're not afraid you're going to hurt me. You're afraid that I'm going to hurt you."

He laughed, cold and hard. "How could I possibly be afraid of you? You are nothing but a waif. I can snap you in half with my hands."

"But you don't. You won't."

"You don't know that." His voice went rough. "I don't know that."

"You do. You know it. You're not afraid you're going to hurt me."

"So confident in your feelings," he said.

"I am confident in that. Because I know you. I do. I know us. Deep down in my soul, Diego, I know who you are. My soul recognizes yours."

"My soul recognizes nothing but my own needs," he said. "And what I need from you right now is not love."

He wrapped his arms around her, lifting her up off the floor and carrying her back toward the bedroom. He undressed, his movements savage, filled with rage. But she knew it wasn't at her. It was at himself. He set her down on the bed, his movements rough, his hands unsteady. "Turn over," he bit out.

"What?"

"Do as I say, *tesoro*. If you want to please me, if you love me, then love me through this. Give me what I actually want. Not words. Your body. Can you love me then?"

It was a dare, and he expected her to fail here. Expected her to turn away.

But she saw him. Saw right through him.

And she would meet him, match him.

He wasn't actually demanding submission as proof of love. He was asking that she prove she could handle his darkness. And he was betting she would not.

But she could.

She obeyed him, turning over onto her stomach, allowing those large, unsteady hands to position her so that she was up on her knees, a pillow propped up beneath her chest. He cupped her, sliding his fingers between her legs, pressing both inside her, testing her readiness. She cried out at the intrusion, feeling almost shameful excitement over the intensity of the moment.

He was trying to make this impersonal. He was trying to kill those feelings that she claimed to have for him. But this... Even his darkness was beautiful to her. Even now he appealed to her body in ways that went beyond logic.

He curved his fingers inside her, stroking some deep pleasure center there she hadn't been aware of before, making her shake and shudder. He smoothed his thumb between the crease of her bottom in time with that motion, pleasuring her there, making her face hot, shock nearly overtaking her pleasure. But not quite.

All she could do was submit to it. Submit to him.

And by the time he positioned his arousal at the entrance to her body, tears were filling her eyes. Because even now, even in his anger, his denial over what was between them, he was working to pleasure her first.

He thrust into her, deep and hard, deeper than he had ever been before, his grip on her hips tight as he rode her roughly, desperately. Like a man trying to exorcise a demon.

She felt it. That desperate need and effort he was putting forward to rid himself of the feelings that he had for her, of the fear. But the harder he pushed, going deeper inside of her even as he tried to get away, the softer she let herself become. She rocked back into him, taking everything he gave, finding a deep, unimaginable power within that decision.

He thought he could use anger to frighten her. He had likely done it all his life. His safety. His protection. That rage that he had learned early on could be so terrifying. But only in the hands of a madman. A sociopath who didn't truly care about anyone or anything but himself. And that was not Diego. Whatever he wished to pretend. It wasn't.

He might have convinced himself, but he would never convince her of that. Fevered, desperate words escaped his lips. Some in Spanish. Some in English. All of them, she had no doubt, profane. But to her, they were a prayer. Because he was fighting a losing battle. One that she would win. One that love would win.

He pressed his hand between her legs, toying with the center of her pleasure as he thrust in deep. And she stopped thinking. Gave herself over completely to the moment. She could feel his anger, almost blinding with its power, could feel his need. In the dark, deep emotion that lived down in the bottom of his heart that he feared more than anything else. His need for love.

"I love you," she whispered, as her pleasure burst

inside of her, white light shining behind her eyelids as her orgasm rocked her.

He growled, a feral denial, even as his body surrendered, as he slammed inside of her one last time and gave himself over to their need.

Then it was done, and they were breathing harshly, both of them reduced by everything that had just happened.

"Liliana…"

"Don't say anything," she said. "Let's not speak."

"Let's go home," he said.

She nodded. "Yes. I want to go home."

CHAPTER ELEVEN

DIEGO DID HIS very best to forget the day of his brother's wedding. And most especially the night that had followed. The way he had taken Liliana back to the penthouse and tried to push her away from him. The way she had clung to him, even while he had played the part of villain in a way that far surpassed his behavior at the wedding.

He didn't understand. He didn't understand how she could know everything she did, about Karina, about the baby, and still say that she loved him. He didn't understand how she remained. It made no earthly sense to him, and yet, while he had been on the verge of sending her away when he had finished making love to her, she had said they should go home.

She had meant the island. The place where he had taken her by force the first time. Home.

As if it were hers too.

And he had been utterly powerless to turn her away. They had not stayed in the penthouse suite. Instead, he'd had his helicopter readied, and the two of them had flown back to the island that very night. They had spent the dusky hours of the morning in bed together, and then when they had arisen, he had found Liliana at the breakfast table eating pastries and looking cheerful, as if none of the previous night had happened.

He didn't know what to do with that. With this woman who stayed.

Who stayed even though she knew exactly what manner of man he was.

He had been an abominable monster to her the night before, and this morning she was just sitting there, un-affected and cheerful.

She looked up at him, her blue eyes shining, her smile brilliant. Did she really love him?

The thought made his stomach turn violently.

And even so, there was a dark, unsavory part of him that thought it was a good thing. If Liliana wanted to lock her own manacles, keep herself prisoner in his world, why shouldn't he let her? He wanted her. He could not foresee a future where he would tire of her or her body. So why shouldn't he have her?

Why shouldn't he allow her to bind herself to him?

"I have been thinking," he said, taking a seat at the table next to her. "I have been thinking that perhaps our agreement is...outdated."

"How do you mean?" she asked, giving him an imp-ish look as she lifted her coffee mug to her lips.

"I am not certain either of us wants this to end."

The smile that earned him lit up her entire face. "No," she said. "I don't."

"Are you certain? Because you were quite enamored with the idea of your freedom..."

"I'm free here," she said. "With you."

"We will not stay here forever. I have houses in major cities all over the world. And that is typically where I conduct my business."

"I'm happy with that," she responded.

"Do you like Paris?" he asked.

"I love Paris."

"London?"

"Yes," she said happily. "I would love living in London for a while."

"We can do that. All of that and more."

She was happy. He was making her smile. He could not recall the last time he had made another person happy. It was so foreign, so unexpected and oddly…satisfying.

He had never much cared for the happiness of another person. Mostly, he had looked to the happiness of himself. Or perhaps *happiness* wasn't even the right word. His own satisfaction. The temporary satiation of his desires, however dark. He had never taken into account what another person might feel. It was just one of the many reasons he had been an awful husband the first time around. One of the many reasons Karina had left him for the sniveling coward she had gone off with. Because at least—by all accounts—he had been a pleasant man.

Even if, in the end, he had been selfish enough to leave his lover to bleed to death on a roadside.

Seeing Liliana's happiness rearranged something inside of him. And he found the corners of his own mouth lifting into a smile. One that lacked cynicism, one that lacked any sort of edge.

He felt her happiness.

That lightness… He felt it in him.

He had been affected by her from the moment he met her, and always, her touch had done something strange to him, something that went beyond the sexual. But this was… This was something else. It was something quite singular.

That moment when she'd come down the stairs in her

wedding gown he'd had that momentary desire to place her up above him and give her whatever she wished.

This, he realized, was the reason for that instinct.

That nothing would ever truly satisfy him except for Liliana's joy.

"Good," he said. "Then it is settled."

"We're married," she said, her smile turning soft and dreamy. "Forever."

The idea didn't terrify him. Not in the least. It was what he had wanted from the moment he had first taken her.

The strength of the obsession that had gripped him from the first moment he'd seen her had been beyond anything he'd ever known, and nothing had come close to dimming it. He doubted time ever would.

There were cursed objects all throughout literature that bewitched men and took hold of their better instincts.

He would call Liliana his own personal cursed object, except...

He was the one who was cursed. And she was simply...

She was everything good and beautiful.

Everything. And he ignored everything inside of him that said it was wrong to know that and claim her anyway. Everything that reminded him that he was the opposite to all that goodness.

He had made her smile. He had made her happy. He could continue to do that. He would.

The important thing was she was his now. She had agreed to it.

And now, he would never lose her.

Liliana was so happy with her new life on the island. With her husband. In the fragile bubble they'd created in this isolated manor, on an isolated island.

It felt so fragile, this little world. Like any intrusion at all might spoil it.

She knew that eventually they were going to have to see how their marriage worked and functioned in the real world, but for now, it was something quite like bliss. For now, she wanted to stay here.

No, he had not said he loved her. But she had known that would be difficult for him. She was prepared to wait. She was prepared to wait for as long as he needed.

She went to sleep with him every night, woke with him every morning, and they shared breakfast. Then, he went off to work, and she set about her day.

She was starting to realize that she wanted to do something with her life. She was no longer living it for the pleasure of someone else. It wasn't like that with Diego. She brought that up with him one night while they were sitting by the fire. She wanted to find her passion, and he had spent the next hour making increasingly ridiculous suggestions about what she might do for a career. And then he had kissed her, brought her down to the ground and told her that of course she didn't actually have to do anything if she didn't want to. She could make her passion his body.

She had told him that of course she was quite passionate about his body, but perhaps needed something to occupy her day.

The next morning at breakfast he had spoken to her about the possibility of her doing freelance editing.

"You love books," he said. "You love to read. Perhaps that would be a good place for you to start?"

"It's more than just reading. With my limited knowledge about how things work, even I know that."

"Certainly, but you're very bright, and I have no

doubt you could learn what you needed to learn to accomplish the job."

"Maybe."

That had started her enrollment in some online classes, in addition to a hefty amount of research.

It was exciting. To think that she was embarking on a whole new part of herself. Husband and a career... Doing something she loved. She had never imagined that she might have those things.

Still, as happy as she was, she found herself feeling weepy and shaky at strange moments. She wondered if it was that impending sense of disquiet that came whenever she thought of them leaving their bubble. Then she wondered if it was nothing more exciting than a little PMS.

Except that was the thing. She was actually quite overdue to have her period.

The realization hit her while she was standing in the middle of her library.

She might be pregnant. And she had no way of finding that out without letting Diego know, because they were the only two people in residence.

She swallowed hard. He would be happy. He had wanted a baby. She worried that it would unearth some bad memories for him, some old grief. But if it did, she would be there.

It was funny that she thought of him, because when she paused for a moment, her own eyes prickled with tears.

She had never known her mother. Her mother had died in childbirth.

She waited for fear that the same fate would befall her, but it didn't come.

She wasn't scared. She never had been, really. Childbirth was dangerous, but with modern medicine, every-thing should be okay. The odds of something happening to her were low, not higher than they were for any other woman, she was sure.

No, she wasn't afraid. But thinking about being a mother when she had never had one…

It was her chance. She could never be the daugh-ter in a mother-daughter relationship. But she could be the mother.

The thought filled her with awe. She pressed her hand to her womb, hoping.

She had been thinking that she and Diego wouldn't have a baby yet, but they were frankly not overly careful with birth control. And with the frequency they made love, it wasn't terribly surprising.

She was happy. Genuinely and truly happy.

She just had to hope it was real.

She walked down the hall quickly, toward Diego's office.

She pushed the door open without knocking, and saw him leaning back in his chair, his feet propped up on the desk. She smiled. She could watch him like this all day. With him not knowing. She loved him. And now they were going to have a family.

"Diego," she said softly.

He turned, a smile on his face, the kind she had been seeing from him more and more. Not those cruel, dark smiles she had seen so often in the beginning. But happiness.

"I'll have to call you back," he said, hanging his phone up. "*Tesoro.* Come in."

"I… I have something to tell you. I think… We'll have to go get it confirmed. But, Diego, I think I'm pregnant."

She couldn't trace all the emotions that flashed through his eyes. "We have to leave," he said. "We need to get you to a doctor."

"I can just have a pregnancy test brought here," she said. "I'm fine."

"That isn't good enough," he responded. "We must get you to a doctor, and we must do it now."

"Diego."

"Your mother died giving birth," he said. "I think that means we should go to a doctor and get you seen."

"You clearly weren't worried about that enough before to use a condom every time you had sex with me."

"I… I didn't think of it."

"You didn't think of pregnancy?"

"I didn't think of your mother," he said.

"Don't worry," she said. "Most women have babies and they're fine."

But he didn't say anything. Instead, he picked up his phone and began to make calls in rapid-fire Spanish, and before she knew it, she found herself bundled up and back on his helicopter, headed toward Spain.

Only a few hours later, she had the results to the test.

And Diego's reaction told her that things between them weren't going to go back to how they were.

She worried they might be broken. Irrevocably. Forever.

CHAPTER TWELVE

HE SLEPT IN his own room that night. He could not possibly sort through all of the feelings in his chest. Liliana was having a baby. *His* baby.

It was not the first time a woman had carried his child.

But this… This was different.

Part of him had wanted this. Had wanted a way to bind her to him. He'd been lax with birth control and he knew it. But it had seemed like a good thing, a way to keep her. But now…

Now something had changed. Something in him, and nothing could have prepared him for the reality of it. He was having all manner of thoughts that hadn't occurred to him before, and they were running through his head on a loop he couldn't stop.

Liliana's mother had died giving birth, and he could not get that out of his head.

His mother had died because of his father.

Liliana's mother by extension had died because of hers. And he just knew. From the moment he had found out she was pregnant he had been gripped by this terrible, awful sense of knowing. He would not be able to keep her. There was no possible way. He had convinced himself that it might be. Had told himself that they could make an arrangement that worked for both of them. And so far, it had been so.

But then there was reality. It was the other shoe, and it had dropped hard.

A child. His child and Liliana's.

After enduring the terror of her being pregnant, the uncertainty of her giving birth, then there would be a child.

And all his past fears rose up around him. The loss of Karina. Of the baby she'd carried.

He couldn't think. His brain was screaming, but it wasn't words. It wasn't anything other than a dark terror that he felt utterly and completely strangled by.

Liliana was having his child. His baby. There was no power in the world he could call upon to protect her.

Because the men in his family lived. They lived and endured, and the women they cared for suffered endlessly.

He knew that she was upset about being sent to her room alone, but it was a kindness, given how he felt.

He couldn't touch her. Not now. Her body was so fragile at the best of times… And now…

He swore, and stomped over to the liquor cabinet, taking out a bottle of vodka and tossing back a solid amount without bothering to pour it into a glass.

That had been his life before Liliana. Drinking. Doing whatever he felt like to keep the demons at bay. To keep the darkness around him a little bit more bearable.

Liliana had given him hope. A hope that he had never deserved.

It was all far too much.

"You're still awake?"

He turned and saw Liliana standing in the doorway. He paused, the bottle poised at the edge of his lips. "Yes."

"Why don't you come to bed?"

"It would be best if I left you alone."

"Don't you think I should be the one to decide that?"

"No, *tesoro*, I don't. I think that my feelings on the matter should come into play."

"We're having a baby, Diego. It's not supposed to be an upsetting thing."

"You say that as if you don't understand why I have concerns."

"I do understand," she said. "I went through my own feelings when I first thought that I might be pregnant. Whether or not I was afraid about my safety. But I'm not."

"That's because you don't remember loss." He took another sip of vodka. "I remember it far too well. More than one."

"But you wanted a child. You wanted to be a father."

"I did," he said, his voice hard. "Because for a moment in time I thought that maybe it could change things. But it didn't."

"You had a tragedy. It wasn't your fault."

"Maybe. Maybe not."

"Come to bed, Diego."

"No," he said.

"You're going to just stay out here and get drunk? What a fine solution to what you apparently see as a terrible problem."

"Do not force the issue, Liliana," he said. "Do not try to talk to me about something you don't understand."

Liliana drew back as if she had been slapped, and he felt a rising tide of guilt. It all felt far too much like his first marriage. Mistakes. His inability to respond correctly at a given moment. He had never felt wrong with Liliana. Even when he had been, taking her from her window. All of it had felt justified. But this felt wrong, and he didn't know what he could possibly do about it.

"Good night," he said.

She nodded slowly, and then turned away from him. And he felt as if she had taken a part of him with her. Peace. A slow-growing peace he hadn't realized had begun to take root inside of him. Gone now that she had turned her back on him.

And so, in the absence of Liliana, in the absence of that peace, he would get drunk.

He didn't know what else to do.

If he was the dark brother, the debauched one, then that was where he would retreat to now.

He didn't know another alternative.

Liliana kept waiting for things to get better. For Diego's smile to return. But there didn't seem to be anything she could do to fix the mood he had fallen into since she'd given him the news of her pregnancy.

He acted as if he was afraid to touch her. Afraid to have any kind of connection with her whatsoever. She felt… She felt defeated.

She had been happy, happy making her life all about finding ways to inject his with hope. With happiness.

Why wasn't that enough? She just wanted to give to him. She didn't understand. Couldn't comprehend why he wouldn't take it. And here they were, back in that same penthouse that had been the source of that hideous fight where they had decided that they were going to make things work between them. Where she had told him that she loved him, and he had said nothing. But it had made him happy—she had been able to see that. She had known it.

Now... Nothing seemed to make him happy at all. His mood was black, and there was no way she could penetrate it.

He had left her alone in the penthouse for the entire day, off to see to some work, he had said. Meanwhile she had set about hatching a plan she'd come up with recently. It had involved no small amount of skulduggery. She had gotten into his things, and thankfully, he had gotten lax, because she was able to get hold of a contact who made deliveries to the island.

And she was able to procure her wedding gown, which she had left back at their house.

With that done, she had set about to collecting all of Diego's favorite foods. She knew what they were, as she had spent the past few weeks grilling him on everything he liked. From music to movies to food. She was determined that her fact-finding mission would pay off.

He hadn't touched her in the days since they'd found out about the baby, and she was suffering for it greatly. She knew he was too. He needed that closeness. That intimacy.

He needed her. She knew he did.

If they could just get back to where they were then things would be better. She could make him happy again.

She could be what he needed. If only he would let her.

Now she had everything arranged. A dinner table with ham, mashed potatoes and a pasta salad. She had fresh baked rolls and a date cake, all of which she had procured in the city. And she was wearing her gown.

He had said that he'd fantasized about tearing it off her, but he hadn't done it.

Perhaps tonight she could bait him into it. Perhaps tonight, they could find their way back to what they'd had.

When the doors to the hotel room opened, she held her breath and stood there, waiting. He walked inside, and his handsome expression froze as he took in the scene that was set before him.

She'd made use of her name as a Navarro and had gotten the hotel concierge to aid her in setting a banquet, a table and two chairs brought up, the table now laden with the food she had gotten.

There were candles, everywhere. It was an extremely romantic scene, if she did say so herself.

But Diego did not look charmed. Not in any way.

"What is this?"

"Dinner," she said, shifting, purposefully moving her hips so that the skirt on the wedding gown swayed.

"How did you get that?"

"Your security is not as tight as it once was," she said dryly.

"I have work to do," he said, breezing past her and heading toward the room he'd been using as an office.

"Don't walk away from me," she said, stamping her foot. "I made dinner for you. Well, I acquired dinner for you. And I expect you to sit with me."

"My apologies, *princesita*. I didn't realize that you were in the position to make demands now."

"You know that I am," she said, walking up to him slowly. She touched his face, sliding her fingertips down, gripping his chin between her thumb and forefinger. "I know you want me. No matter that you're avoiding me now. You can't pretend that you suddenly don't."

"Is that what's bothering you? That I haven't had sex with you?"

"That's just a symptom."

"Perhaps I'm not hungry," he said, his voice cold. "In any of the ways that word might apply."

"I don't believe you."

"That is fine," he said.

Desperation kicked through her chest as he began to pull away from her. "No," she said.

She flung herself at him, wrapping her arms around his neck and kissing him, his lips remaining firm and unresponsive.

She didn't know what she would do if she couldn't reach him. If he didn't need her. She didn't understand why she couldn't make him happy. The man had kidnapped her from her bedroom window so that he could have her and now he was acting like he didn't care at all. She had no idea how she could survive this. How she could endure it. She didn't know what to do to fix it. She had tried. Had tried being everything to him, and he wouldn't take it.

She traced the outline of his lips with her tongue, and he groaned. She felt the exact moment she had breached his control.

"Now's your chance," she whispered against his lips. "Tear this dress off me. Do it like you wanted to then. On the floor. I'm not so fragile, Diego. Do what you need to."

She knew then that she had done it. Because he growled, his hold on her suddenly strong. And then, he grabbed the bodice of her dress and ripped it down violently, the fabric wrenching apart, a glitter of beads spraying everywhere, scattering all over the floor. Leaving her bare, leaving her exposed. Exposing him too.

His movements were dark and rough, and he reduced the dress to nothing but delicate tatters that shimmered like diamonds on the floor.

It felt far too close to how she felt in her soul. Torn, but still hopeful.

His lips were rough on her breasts, his teeth, his whiskers abrading her delicate skin. He gripped her tightly, so tightly she was sure he would leave a bruise. But she didn't mind. She wanted him to. If this was what he needed, she wanted him to expend all of that darkness, in her.

He was hers. It was her job to make him happy. She would do whatever it took. Anything.

If she couldn't do that, then he wouldn't need her. And if Diego didn't need her...

She cried out as he sucked one nipple deep into his mouth, the sound an expression of the desire that was riding through her body, and of the desolation that was echoing in her soul. The very idea of him not needing her, period, of him sending her away.

She closed her eyes tightly, trying to keep the tears from escaping them. She hated this. This feeling of not being able to reach him. Of being separate. She needed him. Needed to connect.

Needed him to love her.

And that was never supposed to be it. It was supposed to be enough that she keep him happy. That should be enough to make her happy. It could be. It would be.

Why did it feel like it wasn't?

A tear rolled down her cheek, and he paused, catching it with the corner of his thumb and brushing it away. When he looked at her, his expression was concerned.

But she didn't want him to worry about her. She wanted to fix him.

So she kissed him, hard and deep. And with every ounce of desperation inside of her. To make him feel what she knew he should.

We are going to have a life together. We're going to have a baby. Please let that be enough for you, please. Please let that be what you want.

She smothered a choked sob as she deepened the kiss, as she let him lift her up off the ground, as she wrapped her legs around him, clinging to him while he lowered them both to the floor.

She jerked his tie loose, ripped open his shirt, moving her hands over as much of his bare chest as she could. While he made quick work of his belt. He opened the front of his pants, not bothering to take any of his clothes off all the way. And he thrust inside of her, deep and hard. His movements erratic and intense. She wanted to take all this, all his rage and his pain and take it down inside her, hold it, take it from him.

She wanted to fix him.

Please. Please. I want to be enough. I want this to be enough.

She didn't realize she'd whimpered that out loud until he caught her lips with his and swallowed the words. And then he was stroking that sensitive place between her thighs, his thumb sliding over her as he thrust home, and she could think of nothing but her own pleasure. She cried out as it crashed over her, as she shook with the power of her orgasm. And he still wasn't done. She felt like she had failed somehow. Like she had been meant to serve him, and had ended up taking her own pleasure so greedily she hadn't done enough. But then he was shouting out his orgasm, and she couldn't worry about it anymore. She just held him.

But when it was over, and he looked down at her, he didn't look better. He didn't look happier.

He looked tortured.

He moved away from her, looking at the casualty of their coming together. "You have to stop this," he said.

"Stop what?"

"You need to be more careful with your body."

"I'm not the one who ravished me on the floor."

"You tempted me," he said. "Don't bait the darkness in me, Liliana. You cannot fix it."

He turned and left her standing there, the table still beautifully appointed with dinner, her dress destroyed in pieces all around her.

"I just want to make you happy," she said.

"You can't," he responded. "I'm not your father for you to spend your life serving, Liliana. You will not find a magic formula to bend me to your will and make me into the man you want me to be. You must stop now. I will not endure it."

"Don't make it sound like that. Like I'm being selfish. I am…giving to you."

"Are you?" he asked, his words like the crack of a whip. "Or are you trying to make me into a tamed thing that you can control as you see fit?"

"I am not."

"Then what is it you're trying to do to me, Liliana?"

"I want to make you happy."

"Why?"

"Because I love you." Desperation clawed at her. "You already know it. Why are you acting surprised?"

"Because I thought you would understand by now, my darling wife, that it doesn't matter how you feel about me. It isn't going to change who I am or how I feel."

"You *need* me," she said.

"I *desire* you," he said. "For a man like me that is a very different thing."

"No," she returned. "It isn't. It isn't that. If it was only desire then you wouldn't still whenever I touched you like you're a spooked horse who needs a gentle hand."

"You vastly underestimate the male libido, *tesoro*. When you put your hand on my arm, I'm imagining it somewhere else on my body. And that is the beginning and end of that."

"Liar."

"You're not the first woman I've been fascinated by, Liliana," he said, his tone sharpening to a knife's edge. "I was married once before—do not forget it. I imagined myself in love with her, but I've since learned the realities of myself. I like soft things. I like beautiful things. And I have never especially cared whether or not they liked me. My wife, Karina, intoxicated me. She fascinated me. Our connection was sexual… It was dark. I wanted that thing she had. That deep, dirty debauchery. I wanted to get it all over me. And I did. But then I did what I do, and the end result was that she was broken."

"Diego…"

"No," he said sharply. "You need to listen to this. You need to listen to me. I saw you, and I wanted your light. All that sweetness. You must understand I don't care if I use it up. I wanted you, and so I captured you. And in the end I will break you too, Liliana. If you allow it. And then I will find the next thing. Because that is the man I am."

"I don't think it's true."

"No. Because you want to change me. You want to

love me so much that I will love you too, because I can't resist the force of it. But isn't that what you spent your entire life doing with your father? And didn't he simply use you as a pawn in the end? Men such as us are what we are. We cannot fight it. And you cannot change it."

"So you're telling me that the best I can hope for in life is to be a discarded husk that lives in your house as your wife and doesn't have your attention?"

"I will not betray our vows. I'm simply telling you what I know to be true about myself."

"Will you fantasize about other women? Wish that it was them because I'll never be enough for you."

"No one and nothing will ever be enough for me, Liliana. Some people are born black holes. And we swallow them. Everything. We take. We don't give. You will not change me, my dear. Love me all you want, but it will never matter." He looked around the room. "Did you think a nice dinner was going to change that?"

She had. She had imagined that if she were good enough, if she were strong enough, made him enough dinners and touched him, kissed him, made love with him when he needed it, that he would love her. That he would need her. She was staring down her very worst fear.

She had fallen for him desperately and she didn't know what she could do to make him—to make him feel the same way. To make him need her like she needed him.

Maybe he'd been right before. Maybe she was trying to turn him into the man she wanted him to be, and not the man he was, for her own ends. Her own comfort.

She loved Diego. But she wasn't sure she knew how to love someone in a way that wasn't this.

And she wasn't making him happy. So what was the

point of it? What was the point of any of this? They could have a baby and not be married. It wouldn't be the end of the world. It wasn't what she wanted, but plenty of people did it.

She blinked back tears as she looked at the table still set with dinner.

She was torturing him. He wasn't happy. And she didn't know what she could do to fix it.

She needed to leave, but she didn't have anywhere to go. Even the very idea filled her with a strange kind of desolation.

Her life had been so much about her father, and now Diego, and beyond the two of them, she had nothing. No connections.

No friends.

She was about to have a baby and she...

She was going to pour all her love into that baby the way that she had done for Diego and her father.

And she wasn't having a sudden crisis where she realized she wanted to live her best life or be more selfish but...

She felt like she needed to know some things about herself. About what she wanted, what she was made of.

What she wanted beyond making someone else happy, because she had no idea how to make Diego happy if she couldn't even figure herself out.

She needed to make herself happy.

She'd never even tried to do that. She'd always gone with what she was told. And even going with Diego...

She hadn't taken responsibility for it. It had been something she'd wanted, but protecting her father's reputation had played a part in it. As had a kidnapping, which she had not chosen.

She wanted Diego. But she needed...

She needed to go. She needed to make a choice.

"I need to go," she said, looking around at the remains of her dress.

"What?"

"I need to go," she said again, striding off toward her bedroom. She began to dress herself quickly, ignoring Diego standing there in the doorway.

Once she was decent, she took her purse and started to march toward the door. Diego caught her arm. "Where do you think you're going?"

"Away from you," she said, jerking her arm back and breezing out the door, shocked when he didn't follow.

She got in the elevator, stabbing at the buttons with numb fingers.

She spent the entire elevator ride down to the lobby blinking back tears. She stumbled across the marble floor, headed toward the double doors, only dimly aware that she had no idea where she was going. Or who would take her there.

But, she supposed that finding a driver to take her to a destination was not as important as finding the destination itself.

"Liliana!"

She turned around to see Diego push open the doors to the elevator that was next to the one she had taken down, his expression wild, his dark hair in his eyes. "Where do you think you're going?"

"I'm leaving," she responded.

"Come back up to our room," he said. "Let us discuss this like reasonable people."

She remembered what he had said at the wedding reception. How he had wanted to talk about the allegations that had been made against him in public. And she had told him no. That they would take their business back to their private space and deal with it between the two of them.

But that wasn't what she wanted. Not now. If he wanted to make a scene, then she would make one. She had been…so well behaved. All her life. She had tried so hard to be good, and it had gotten her nowhere. She had been the best daughter her father could have possibly wanted or asked for and it had never earned her a damn thing. All it had gotten her was an arranged marriage, and then he had…

He had left her with her kidnapper. Had told her to marry him to protect his reputation.

That wasn't the action of a man who loved her. Nothing that she had done had managed to accomplish that. And then there was Diego. She had done her best to make him happy. She had given and given. She had promised to stay with him. She had worn the wedding dress he had picked out, had given him all of herself.

And what had he given her in return? She was eternally hoping that if she threw herself over the top of the sacrificial altars that eventually someone would halt the execution and spare her out of a sense of great love. But no. They just sacrificed her. Again and again.

She had to want more. She had to be more.

"Do you love me?" she shouted.

They were drawing looks from both the hotel staff and the guests, but she didn't care.

"Liliana," he said, his tone warning.

"No," she said. "It's a simple question, and it shouldn't be difficult for you to answer. Do you love me?"

He looked around, and then seemed to decide that he didn't much care what anyone thought either. "Is that suddenly a requirement for you?"

"Yes. I want you to stop hiding. Stop hiding behind that 'broodier than thou' thing. I'm sorry that your wife died. I'm sorry that she left you. I'm sorry that your mother's dead. And that your father is an unrepentant asshole."

"He's a dead unrepentant asshole," Diego said dryly.

"Well. I'm sorry about that too, just because it means you can't torture him to death. But there's nothing you can do about any of it. There's nothing I can do about any of it. You are the one that's deciding to be unhappy."

"I never said happiness was a goal, Liliana," he said.

"Why isn't it?" she shouted. "Why isn't it a goal? We could be happy. We could be. Together. We're having a baby. I love you. Why isn't that enough for you?"

"What is it you want from me? You want me to make you my entire life? You want me to entrust my happiness to you? Look at you," he said. "You're such a fragile thing. So easily broken, and you want me to embrace a potential future with you and assume nothing will ever happen? You live in a fantasy world, Liliana. I knew that you were innocent, but I had no idea that you were this innocent."

"What are you saying exactly? That you can't love me? Or that you won't love me?"

"It doesn't make a difference," he said. "I'm not a man who wants love. Not anymore. Perhaps there was a time when I would have. But that time is past."

"So a dead woman who betrayed you gets to be your only attempt at being in love, and I get left out in the cold even though I'm carrying your child, and I'm practically down on my knees begging you to love me?"

"You're not on your knees, *tesoro*. But, if you wanted to go ahead and make that a literal truth, I'm not opposed to it."

"You wouldn't want me to beg," she said. "That isn't what you want or need. You need someone to stand up to you and tell you that you're not scary. The only person terrified of you is you. And that's because you're terrified of the fact that there might actually be hope living inside of that granite chest of yours. It's not your darkness that scares you—it's the light. The light that won't go out no matter how many times you tell yourself and other people it isn't there. In your heart, you want to love me. You want to love this baby. All of that stuff that you say about wanting to keep me, the way that you quiet when I put my hands on you… Diego, you love me."

"I don't," he said, his face horribly blank.

He was scared—she knew that he was. She knew better than to take his word as truth. At least, she was hoping it was a lie. If it wasn't, she didn't know what she would do. She was trying to be strong, trying to stand there and cling to the realizations she had had only moments before, but it was so hard. So hard when she just wanted to fold herself into his arms and tell him it didn't matter if he loved her. That she would give him whatever he wanted as long as they could be together.

But she needed more than that. She had to demand more than that for herself, no matter how difficult it was.

Because what she had just said to Diego was true in the end. He would not love a woman who got on her knees and begged. If he had wanted a captive, he would have kept her a captive. If he had wanted someone weak and wilting, he wouldn't have boosted her strength over the course of the past few weeks. He wouldn't have latched on to their banter, rewarded her sharp comments with witty banter of his own.

If she wanted him to love her, then she had to be herself. Not the creature her father wanted to shape her into. Not the woman she had been imagining she could be for Diego. That was the real test.

When they had made love the night of the wedding, she had imagined that because she had been created for him that meant taking on board his endless darkness if necessary and asking for nothing in return. But the fact of the matter was, he didn't want her to just give. Not only that. He would want her to push too. To pull. She had to trust that she was made for him not simply when she was being accommodating, but when she was demanding more from him. When she was standing up for herself, for him, for all that he could have. When she was telling him things he didn't want to hear and demanding what he wasn't ready to give.

"Coward," she said.

"What?"

"You heard me," she said, taking a reckless step forward, crashing into a potted plant and sending it falling sideways, the ceramic shattering, soil spreading everywhere on the white floor. It hadn't looked like an accident. It looked like she was having a tantrum. She didn't care. She just didn't care.

"You're a coward. You could love me, but you're scared to. And you can give any reason you want, but that doesn't make it true. You're trying to protect yourself. Maybe you should think about someone else. About what they want. About what they need."

She turned away from him. "Wait," he said. "You can't leave me."

"I have to leave you," she said. "Because if I don't, then I am going to be that wilting, sad girl that you met living at her father's house, willing to marry whatever

man he handed her over to when she really wanted another one."

"If you really wanted me that whole time, then why
won't you take me now?"

"Because I need more. I need more than you at your
worst, Diego. I can love you through it, but I shouldn't
have to live with it for my entire life. Not when you can
be more. More for me. More for our child. I'm going to
leave. And I'll probably love you that whole time, but I
need to be somewhere else. To be better for our child.
To be better for me."

"You can't go," he said. "I won't allow it. I will chase
you down to the ends of the earth. I will ruin your father with all the evidence I have against him. I will…
I will have our child taken from you."

She drew back, feeling as though he had struck her,
and he continued to advance on her. "Do not test me,
Liliana," he said. "You will not like the consequences."

"If you won't allow me to be happy with you, Diego,
then I beg you allow me to be happy somewhere. You
might choose to live in the darkness, but I'm not doing
that. I'm sorry if that diminishes your bank account,
Diego, but as you refuse to care for me, that's all that
will be left diminished."

"So in the end you are just like Karina."

"No," she said. "I'm not leaving with another man.
I'm not leaving to hurt you. I'm leaving on my own.
I'm leaving to heal me. In the end, I hope it heals you
too. But if not… I can't live solely for someone else for
the rest of my life. And you wouldn't like the woman I
became if I did. Let me go. If you have any humanity
in you at all, let me go."

Then she turned and walked outside into the night.
And she waited. Waited for him to follow after her.

Waited for him to wrench the doors open and call her name as he had done in the lobby. But he didn't.

She called a cab, and on her way to the airport used that same contact she had used to get the ill-fated wedding gown collected. She figured out a way to find a new place to stay. Then after boarding a private plane using her husband's name, she landed in London several hours later, and procured lodging using her father's name.

And she decided that whatever she did after that, she would use her own name. She couldn't figure out how to be enough for Diego. But maybe… Maybe she could figure out how to be enough for herself. And if she could do that… Then maybe she had a hope of being a good mother. Of being a whole, happy person.

The rest… Her broken heart, her need for Diego… She would worry about that later.

She laughed ruefully in the empty hotel room. Tonight, she had kidnapped herself, in a way. Taken herself out of that life that she had built with him, so that she could find something else.

Because if she didn't, the kind of despair that she felt after he abandoned her would be all she really had.

And she was beginning to discover that she needed to find more.

The revelations she'd had at the hotel, that continued to unfold on her flight to London, were the kinds of self-realization that settled in her stomach like rocks. She didn't feel lighter. Didn't feel magically healed. But still, she couldn't ignore them. That she didn't know how to be with someone without constantly trying to fill the gaps. Without constantly trying to make herself invaluable.

She needed to fix that. And when she did, maybe she would feel better.

But for now she was lost in the in-between. Where she knew what she needed to become, but felt miles and miles away from it, when all she wanted to do was lie on the ground, curl up into a ball and howl.

And since she was by herself, that was what she did.

CHAPTER THIRTEEN

DIEGO COULDN'T FATHOM what had possessed him to simply stand in that hotel lobby while Liliana walked out of his life. While the people around him practically cheered at her strength, clearly taking her side in the matter.

And why wouldn't they?

She'd asked if he loved her. He'd told her no.

And then she'd begged him to let her go. Her eyes had been full of tears, her voice heavy with pain, and he'd... He'd done it because what other choice had there been?

She was miserable. He could see it in her eyes. She was breaking apart right in front of him, and he... He cared. He had never cared about anyone else like this in his life. Not since his mother's death.

She was gone. She was gone, and he should continue to allow it. He should let her go. Because she wanted and needed more than he could give.

That thought stunned him. He had never cared before what someone else wanted or needed. Always, his whole life it had been about himself.

About surviving.

He gritted his teeth, thinking about that moment when he had set his father's shop on fire. Thinking that certainly he would have tempted the old man to murder.

And all he could think was that Matías had somehow sidestepped this. That his brother was married and his wife…

He didn't know how to have it. He didn't understand. He was far too broken to have this. To have her.

Here he was nearly prostrate on the ground in a penthouse in Spain, while his brother was likely off honeymooning.

He picked up his phone, weighing it in his hand for a moment before dialing his assistant. "Find out where my brother is," he said.

"Yes, Mr. Navarro."

A few moments later his phone rang. "He's at his office in London."

Diego hung up the phone. He wondered why his brother was at his office, rather than at the *rancho* enjoying his new wife's body. It's what Diego would be doing if he hadn't sabotaged his entire life.

He needed to talk to Matías. It was the one thing he hadn't done. Beyond their thinly veiled threats made to each other when he had taken Liliana.

Diego had let Liliana go. And for the first time in longer than he could remember, he felt hope. She had changed him. Only two months ago he would never have released her. Not ever. He had taken her not giving a damn whether she wanted to be with him or not. Had forced her into marriage the same way. But something in him had changed. She had changed and he needed to…

He needed to know. How Matías had done it. How he was a good man. He needed to be a better one, for Liliana.

Liliana.

He thought of her, so brave and bright, facing him down and calling him a coward. She wasn't wrong.

No. She wasn't.

His phone rang, and he answered it, his heart in his throat. It was his assistant.

"Your brother has a message for you, Mr. Navarro."

"Does he?" Diego asked.

"He says it's all yours."

What was all his? Diego couldn't think straight for a moment. Everything wasn't his, or Liliana would be here. But she wasn't. So it couldn't be.

The inheritance.

Which meant...

Which meant all was not bliss with Matías and Camilla. Did that mean that there wasn't hope after all? Or did it mean Matías wasn't magically good?

If that was the case, did it mean Diego wasn't beyond help?

"I need a plane to London," Diego said. "Immediately."

There were some things that needed to be handled in person, and this, Diego had a feeling, was one of them.

When Diego walked into his brother's high-rise office, Matías was standing in front of his desk, a panoramic view of London behind him, two drinks in his hand and a smile on his face.

"You would only smile when offering me a drink if it was poisoned," Diego said, reaching into his jacket and pulling out a flask for his brother to see. "I'm good."

Matías normally looked...

Diego and his brother had many features in common. Both over six feet tall with black hair, dark eyes and strong noses. But Matías always looked at ease with his surroundings, and as a result, people in his presence always seemed at ease. Diego had the opposite effect. Creating waves wherever he went.

But today... Today there was no easy way about his brother at all.

"To what do I owe the displeasure?" Matías asked.

"I heard that you had forfeited our little game," Diego said.

"Because it quit being a game to me."

"Oh, I see. So it was still a game when I stole Liliana right out of her bedroom, but it's not a game now. Fascinating."

The bastard. He hadn't called it off when Liliana had been taken. The very idea of his brother marrying Liliana when he cared so little for her made Diego's stomach turn.

"Liliana said that she wanted to be with you," Matías pointed out. "I was hardly going to rescue a woman who didn't wish to be rescued."

"Yes," Diego said. "She did tell you that. Because I'm blackmailing her. Her father is not the upstanding citizen that he appears to be, and Liliana was quite shocked to find out the Hart family name was not built on the pristine foundation she had once thought. A tragedy all around."

"Not for you, though."

"Indeed," Diego said, "I have met very few tragedies that I didn't want to exploit. And this was no different. However," he said, "I think it is time we finish this."

It was another thing he could do. The last easy thing, he realized. He needed to make sure there was no external benefit to him being with Liliana. If he were going to go after her...

There was some deep work he had to do. Inside his very soul, and that would be difficult. But this... This he could do.

"I agree," Matías said. "And you've won."

"No," Diego said. "Abuelo has won. At least if we allow him to." His brother rubbed his chin thoughtfully, then took a drink from his flask. "So, you wish to discontinue this, to call your marriage a sham and be done with it. I wish to do the same."

Matías could only stare at his brother. Shocked at the words he'd just spoken. "Why?"

"I suspect for the same reasons you do," Diego said, taking a drink from his flask. "It got away from you, didn't it?"

He was desperate for the answer. Desperate to know if he was alone in this or if Matías was similarly afflicted. And what the hell his brother, the better man by all accounts, was going to do about it.

"Has it gotten away from you?" Matías looked surprised.

"Liliana Hart," Diego said, "was supposed to be the simplest and softest of targets. I have watched her for years while doing business with her father. Sheltered. Meek, or so I thought. She is such an innocent, Matías, you have no idea. At least, she was."

Diego felt like his heart was being squeezed even as he spoke of her like that. But it was the truth. He'd imagined her a piece of light he could capture easily. A lightning bug he could keep in a jar and claim for his own without consideration.

But Liliana wasn't meek. She wasn't soft or breakable. She was a force.

She damn well might have broken him.

"So, neither of us play?" Matías asked. "That's what you're proposing?"

"Yes," Diego responded. "I already called Grandfather and told him that Liliana was divorcing me."

"Is she?"

"I have already put her on a plane back to America. Along with all of the evidence of her father's misdeeds so that she has no fear I will use it against her."

"We are in a similar place, then. As I have sent Camilla away. Back to her family *rancho*, and have just finished procuring documents for her to sign that will restore ownership."

Diego laughed darkly. Then he reached out and grabbed hold of the whiskey tumbler in Matías's hand. He took a drink, quick and decisive. It burned all the way down. He hoped it would blot out some of the pain that he felt. It didn't.

"I thought you were afraid that was poisoned," Matías pointed out.

"At this point, I feel it would be all the same either way."

Matías shrugged, and took a sip of his own whiskey. "You may not be wrong."

"I have always found it astoundingly simple to take what I want," Diego said. "Why was it not with her?"

Matías sighed heavily, his gaze on the wall behind Diego. "You're not going to like my conclusion."

"Oh, probably not." Diego didn't like anything about this. Why should he like his brother's conclusions?

"Love."

The word was like a dagger straight through his heart. It was all that he wanted. All that he feared.

"I've already tried love," Diego said. "Against my better judgment."

But he hadn't loved Karina. Not really. He'd seen the chance for oblivion in her and he'd taken it. But he hadn't loved her.

"It ended badly," Matías said.

"Yes," Diego answered slowly, "though not in the way that people think."

"I knew that already."

The two brothers stared at each other for a moment. They had never been close. The way they had grown up had simply made it impossible. Diego had acted out. He'd made himself into a man that Matías would never want to speak to, much less spend any time with.

His brother had always wanted to escape the kind of debauchery their father had reveled in, and Diego had played on the outskirts of it. Why would Matías want to be close with him?

Maybe that had been the whole point. To push him away. To not risk anything with his brother. To not ever be close with another living soul because loss hurt too badly.

Maybe it was time to try. To talk about something they never had. If they could do that, if they could deal with that hideous childhood they'd both managed to survive, maybe they could take a step toward a different life.

Diego hadn't imagined Matías needed that, but now he wondered. He'd lost his wife, the same as Diego had lost his.

"I know that our father killed our mother," Diego said, his tone grave.

"Dios," Matías said. "Why did you never say?"

"I don't know how to talk about such things," Diego said. "And he…threatened me. And as a boy I was too frightened to stand against him. I am a coward, Matías, and I have to live with that."

"You were a child, not a coward."

Diego went on as though Matías hadn't spoken. "And I know that… That I am broken. Just as he was."

"No," Matías said, the denial so swift and fierce it shocked Diego. "You're not. He was. Abuelo is. We can be something else."

"Can we?"

"Does Liliana love you?"

I love you. Don't you love me?

"I don't think so."

How could she? How? It didn't make any sense. He was the monster who'd kidnapped her, and then denied her love when she gave it freely. She'd asked to be let go, and he'd obliged. The only good thing he'd ever done for her.

But if she still could…

"Camilla says she loves me. And I feel that… I feel that if she can love me then perhaps I'm not broken."

"The concern," Diego said, his voice rough, "becomes breaking them."

"Yes," Matías agreed. "But I wonder… If love is the difference."

"That is the one thing I can confidently say our father and grandfather do not possess at all. Though, that highlights other failures of mine, sadly."

"No one ever taught us how to love, Diego," Matías said. "They taught us to be ruthless. They taught us to play these games. To be cold, unyielding men who cared for nothing beyond our own selfish desires."

"I would say they taught us everything we should have tried not to be. And you," Diego said, "have certainly come the closest."

"I still didn't have love. So I'm not sure if it made any difference in the end."

"Is it too late now? Do you think it's too late to have it now?"

He wished it weren't. He needed it not to be. He'd

lived half his life convinced his fate was set in stone, but maybe it wasn't. Maybe… Maybe he could change.

He'd let her go.

He wanted her to be happy.

He wanted her to know he chose her.

He didn't want money.

He didn't want to win.

If all those things could change, then maybe there was no limit to it. Maybe he could be whatever she needed. Maybe they could have any life they chose.

"It's never too late," he said. "I have to believe that. And then, even when it is too late, I feel that you have to keep trying. Beyond hope. Beyond pride or reason. Because love has no place in any of those things. Love is something entirely different."

"When did you become such an expert?" Diego asked.

"I'm not," Matías said. "But I know about pride. I know about failing. I know about loss. I know about selfishness. I know about anger. And nowhere, in any of that, did I find peace. Nowhere was there love. I can only assume it's this thing," he said, "this thing that feels foreign, this thing that I don't know at all. This thing that has taken me over, body and soul. And… I wanted. I would've given it all up for her. We were both acting fools for this, and we were willing to give it up for them. Would our father have ever done that?"

"No," Diego said, without hesitation.

"No," Matías agreed.

"Well then," Diego said. "Perhaps we are not broken after all."

Whether or not he could take the chance on breaking Liliana was another thing entirely.

CHAPTER FOURTEEN

SHE WAS DOING well in her online classes, so there was that. Liliana imagined that she should feel triumphant that she had managed to move forward with her plans, even with her heart nothing more than ground-up shards of glass in her chest. But it was difficult to feel pride around all the pain inside her.

She was becoming her own woman, and she was finding that it was not the easiest thing. It was going to take some doing before she was able to pay for her own lodging. Well, it would take less doing if she moved out of the city. London was obviously going to be impossible for a pregnant student earning freelance money. At least, it would be impossible for her to get herself into any neighborhood that didn't make her feel she was in danger at all times.

She supposed she could get roommates. And that was definitely a route she was considering taking.

But for now, she was just still hiding away in one of her father's properties.

He had no idea she was there. He owned far too many places to notice that one, pale blonde was holed up in any of them.

She wondered if Diego had been in touch with him. If he had threatened him.

Diego must be furious. It had all occurred to her later that of course she had destroyed his chance at getting his family inheritance.

She almost felt guilty.

But...

She couldn't worry about him, and she couldn't live for him.

Oh, her heart still beat for him, but her actions needed to be for more.

She needed to be more.

If there was one thing she had done a lot of over the past few days, it was think about the future. Her future as a mother. She didn't know what a mother was supposed to do, not beyond what she had seen in TV, movies and read in books. She'd never had a mother. And her father had been such a difficult parental figure.

She had made quite a few decisions about what she wanted to be.

She was not going to expect her child to live for her. She couldn't put that on another person. She knew what it was like. To have someone care for you only as long as you were a vehicle for their goals.

But she had to be strong for her child, otherwise they would inevitably feel a sense of obligation. That meant she had to find her happiness in more than just motherhood, though she knew she would find so much joy in it. It wasn't for herself. It was for that child. Because if she didn't make a concerted effort, with just her and the baby she would put far too much on that little one's shoulders.

She didn't want to do that.

Didn't want to hurt people in the ways that she had been hurt.

And while she had been musing on that she realized

that the way she had loved Diego had actually done that very same thing to him.

If he didn't react in the right ways, if he didn't look happy when she wanted him to be happy, she was putting her expectation of fulfillment on him. Which, for all he had done, he had never done that to her. It was she who had done that herself. Diego was not like her father. But while hers manifested themselves in a much more altruistic way, she did have some similar tendencies.

She wanted Diego to be happy with her love because she wanted to feel good about herself. And that made it a somewhat selfish love.

Her father had said to her so many times that she was all he had, and there had been any number of addendums to that. She was all he had, and so she had to stay with him. So she had to be a good daughter. So she had to help him, because he needed her.

Diego had to be happy because she loved him. Diego had to love her so that she would feel good.

Yes, it might be different, it might come from a less manipulative place, but it was the same.

She was trying to figure out how she could want those things for him without imposing herself on him. And the only thing she could think was by being away like this. He would want to see his child, that much she knew. They would have to contend with each other eventually. But perhaps… Being forced to contend with each other as people, as parents, would be better.

She wanted less self-realization and more bread. Bread was all she wanted to eat. The craving was as real as it was intense. And her body didn't mind overmuch what kind of bread it was. Buttered and toasted brioche in the morning, a baguette and some cheese in the afternoon, a pastry in lieu of dinner. Just carbohydrates and fats.

She couldn't have love, so perhaps she could have butter, and that seemed about the best substitute she could manage.

With no small amount of guilt, she was using her father's means to procure food as well. Living at his address meant she was able to charge whatever she liked as long as it was delivered to the penthouse. She was awaiting her afternoon baguette, coupled with the evening's cinnamon roll. She was suddenly starving, and she had a feeling she would be eating everything all at once.

When the buzzer sounded, she immediately granted access and sat down on the couch, waiting. She felt like she was in the strangest emotional space she'd ever been in. Ready to be more independent on the one hand. And yet, nearly useless on the other. Lying around and allowing food to be delivered to her while she lounged on a couch.

Maybe it was hormonal. Maybe it was heartbreak. Maybe it was a unique combination of the two.

She would muscle past it eventually. She just didn't want to yet.

She didn't have the heart to yet.

The door opened. "Just set it on the table," she said.

"So very imperious," came a dark voice from behind her. "I assume you mean the bread."

She jerked upright into a seated position. "Why do you have my bread?"

"The deliveryman downstairs was more than happy to allow me to bring it up to my wife."

"Well, that doesn't seem very professional. He has no way of verifying that you're my husband."

"Don't you have other questions? Like how I found you and why I'm here?"

"I'm hungry," she said, her heart beating rapidly, her hands beginning to shake. "My concerns are centered around my lunch."

"Then have your lunch, *tesoro*," he said, handing her the paper bag that contained the baguette. But in truth, she was no longer hungry at all.

She clutched the bag to her chest, using it as some sort of defense. Against what, she didn't know. Maybe just the sheer force of him. Of all that he was.

He was still the most beautiful man she had ever seen. He called to her. Made her ache. Made her need.

All the grand plans for independence she had made felt diminished.

No. They weren't diminished. That was the wrong way to think of it. She could stand on her own. She has been doing it for the past few days. She was confident she could do it for as long as she needed to. But she wanted to lean into his strength. There was the life she could endure, and there was the one that she wished for. What she knew about herself now was that she could make hard choices. She could do what needed to be done. But she would rather… Oh, how she would rather have a life with him.

"I have brought you something," he said.

She crinkled the bread bag. "I know. I'm holding it."

"There is something other than bread in the bag, Liliana."

She rustled into the brown paper, and found a folder containing a stack of documents.

"What is this?"

"Proof," he said, "of your father's misdeeds. All the proof that I have. Beyond exploiting the connections to the people that I know, this is the only written proof that there is. It is yours now. You're free. I'm not going to use it against you. I'm not going to use it against him."

"Why?"

"Because you don't have to be with me, Liliana."

"What about your inheritance?"

"I forfeited it. As did my brother."

"What...? What's going to happen with that? What will your grandfather do?"

"That is up to him. I informed him that you left me. He wanted to know why I didn't simply force you to return, as I had kidnapped you once. I told him that forcing you to be with me no longer appealed."

"It doesn't?"

"And I need you to understand that. I need you to understand that I... I have never cared what another person wanted or felt, Liliana. The decision to kidnap you was an easy one. I wanted you, and I saw no reason I should not have you. I just didn't care what you wanted. I didn't care if you loved Matías, if you were his lover. It didn't matter to me."

He advanced on her, his eyes full of fire. "But when you asked me to let you go at the hotel... I cared. What you wanted mattered to me. And it has, Liliana, for weeks. But that was the first moment that what you wanted mattered more than what I wanted. Because what I wanted to do was chase you down in the streets and haul you back upstairs. To remind you that you're mine. To remind you that you wanted to be with me, no matter what. But I knew I couldn't force you, because suddenly your happiness meant more than my satisfaction. It has never mattered to me. I am not one of those altruistic men who avoided connections in order to spare people their darkness. You know I didn't. I married once, and the fallout was horrific, and still, I took you. Still, I wanted to marry you. And then it changed."

"How?"

"I don't know," he said, his voice rough. "I only know that the moment I realized that, the moment I let you walk away, was both the darkest and brightest moment I've had in years. Losing you, letting you go, was hell on earth. But realizing that I could change…"

"Of course you can change," she said. "Anyone can. We've changed each other, Diego. That first moment I saw you something in me changed, and in all the time since, it has only been made stronger. The fact that I was able to walk away from you was a change in me. I've spent my life only understanding a strange kind of codependent love. And I… It's the strangest thing, Diego. But I realized two things. Not only that the way I loved you wasn't fair to me. But that it wasn't fair to you. I cannot subject you to a life where my happiness is dependent on you reacting the way I want you to. To every little thing. That isn't fair. And you're right. It is me trying to control you to make you safer. To make you easier to deal with. I imagined that it was a giving, selfless love, but it isn't. It's just martyrish, and it isn't fair. You never asked for a martyr. But there I was, more than willing to play the part. And now… I would be okay, if we couldn't be together. I could stand on my own feet. I would figure it out. I'm going to find a way to not need my father's money. To not need yours."

"Well, that is extremely good to hear, *tesoro*. It sounds as if you don't need me to survive. And I don't need you to fulfill my dark purposes. There is now no more blackmail. So it seems to me that there is only one thing left."

"What is that?"

"Choice. It is the one thing both you and I seem to have been afraid of all this time. If it's all the world, if it's fate, if it's duty, then the pain that results is not ours, is it?"

"I don't suppose it is."

"If I am simply destined to be my father, then as much guilt and blame as I take on for our failed marriage, it's still hollow. Because I'm blaming my blood. Not the choices that I made that brought me there."

"If I am the daughter my father wants me to be, then when I find myself unhappy with the choices that were made for me..."

"You blame him."

"And if my husband blackmailed me into marriage, kidnapped me out of the bedroom window... I suppose when times get hard I can blame him as well."

"Yes. And when I find myself resisting loving my wife because the very idea terrifies me, then I can blame the loss in my childhood. The manner of man my father was. All the failures that have come since. It is so much easier to cling to the past and use it as a scapegoat than it is to move on to the future and realize that everything that happens from here on out... It will be my choice."

"Yes," she said softly.

"I chose to let you go. The first choice that defied what I considered to be my nature."

"I chose to walk away."

"And so now here we are again," he said. "With choices to make."

"And what choice have you made, Diego?"

He shocked her then, dropping to his knees in front of the couch, taking hold of her hands. "I choose you, Liliana. You said that I was your light, when all I saw in myself was darkness, but that too is a matter of choice.

I want to be your light. I want to love you, even though it is hard for me."

She pulled back slightly, her heart twisting. Hard to love her? She didn't know quite what to do with that.

He reached up and cupped her cheek. "No, don't mistake me. It is not hard to love you. It is hard for me to accept that I do. Because what terrifies me most is all that I cannot control. All that love costs. All that loss can cause a man to endure."

"Well. It's scary," she said, pressing her hand over his, holding his palm to her face.

He looked down. "But the real failing in my first marriage was not that I am like my father. It was that I married someone I never intended to give myself to completely. I convinced myself that as long as I was faithful that was all there was to it. As long as I didn't murder my wife, then perhaps I was better than my father, but I had a conversation with my brother. And we both realized something."

He looked up, his dark eyes meeting hers. "Love is the difference. Love is what makes you choose someone else's happiness over your own. Love makes walking away from your family inheritance seem easy. Love makes letting go of fear seem worth it. Love is what makes you a better man. A better person. And love is what I have found with you. Fear held me back. It made me want to push you away. Running from love made me say things I deeply regret. Made me treat you in a way I should not have. But now I'm before you, kneeling. As I wanted to do that first moment I saw you in your wedding gown. You are my queen, Liliana. The queen of my heart. And I am begging you give me a chance. I no longer want to own you. I simply want to love you."

She touched his face, tilting his chin up so that his eyes met hers. "I love you," she said. She set the bag down, and slid off the couch, so that she was on her knees with him. So that neither of them were above or below the other. "You are my king," she said. "The ruler of my heart. And you do hold me captive, but as long as I hold you, it will all be right in the end."

"I think I loved you from the first moment I saw you," he said. "But it took a great effort on my part to attempt to deny it while also trying to bring you into my possession. I suppose I can only be grateful that Matías intended to take you as his bride, because it pushed me to act sooner than I might have."

"Are you so afraid now? About the baby?"

"I'm more terrified than I have ever been in my life," Diego said. "Because I love more in this moment than I ever have. I love my life. I love you. I love my vision of our future, and with that comes…fear. Of all that I cannot control. But know this, Liliana. That which is in my power to do, I will do."

"I don't need you to control the whole world, Diego. I just need you to love me."

"I do. I will."

"I knew it," she said, leaning in and kissing him on the mouth.

"What did you know?"

"That we were made for each other. That if I trusted in that we would find our way here. I think we could have stayed together as we were. But it wouldn't have been this. It wouldn't have been everything."

"Thank you," he said. "For trusting in that, even when I could not."

"I'll trust in it forever," she said. "In our love."

"I trust in our love too. And more than that, in that

the moment I met you, my soul recognized yours. Recognized his other half.

"You're the light to my darkness," he said.

She smiled. "And isn't it funny, how you're the light to mine."

"I think, *tesoro*, that that is exactly how it should be." His lips curved, still pressed against hers. "It was never the inheritance," he said.

"What?"

"The real reason I wanted you. It was never the inheritance, Liliana. It was always you. The rest was an excuse."

"Really?"

"Yes," he said. "You were always the true treasure, my love. Always."

EPILOGUE

WHEN HIS SON made his entrance into the world, Diego Navarro was overwhelmed by a sense of relief and joy. The birth was easy. Everyone said so, even Liliana, who seemed surprised by how smoothly it had all gone.

Diego, for his part, had left nothing to chance. He had hired the best team of doctors in the world, had installed her in the plushest delivery suite available from the moment her first contraction had hit two days before the actual birth.

But now he was here, his son.

And so was his wife. The love of his life. The center of his whole world.

His grandfather had already called with his gift for the child. The inheritance. Part of Diego wanted to reject it, and he himself might not take any of it. But for his son... He would allow it for his son. And as for Matías, it meant that his brother could keep the *rancho*, which he loved. And Diego was more than happy to let his brother have full ownership of all that was his.

He no longer felt compelled to chase after the darkness inside of him. Not when Liliana's light had done so much to drive it out.

"What should we name him?" Liliana asked, gazing down at their precious boy.

"I don't know," he said.

"Is there no family name you want to use?"

For them, family would never be the blood that had made them. Liliana had given all the evidence of her father's wrongdoings to the women who had been harassed by him, and they had set about dismantling the legacy he'd built on so much corruption.

There had been no reconciliation possible for them after that.

But they were family. A family that was growing, with love that would grow right along with it.

"No," he said decisively. "I want our family to start with us. We are new. Because of our love. We are not tied to any legacy."

"No," she said, smiling slowly. "We are not. I do have a suggestion, though."

In the end, they named him Matteo Navarro. In honor of Matías, who Diego had always seen as the best of their blood. And more than that, as a man who could change, a man who could love, even when it was hard. And in the end, it was his talk with Matías that had helped him win back Liliana.

"Matías and I are the beginning. You and Camilla are the beginning," Diego said.

"Yes. That is true," Liliana said. "Though, I think that love is the beginning."

Diego Navarro spent all his life making a very good habit of loving his children, loving his wife.

It started with the first moment he set eyes on Liliana. When the flames that had always been inside of him had seen her and leaped upward, toward destruction, he had thought.

He had thought that fire in him meant he was lost, but she'd taught him different. It could do terrible damage, there was no doubt about that. But love made the difference. It was love that made it burn bright enough to light the way. That made it burn hot enough to keep them warm, but not so hot it destroyed.

Love, he had learned, made all the difference in the world.

* * * * *

LET'S TALK

Romance

For exclusive extracts, competitions
and special offers, find us online:

- ⨍ facebook.com/millsandboon
- ⌾ @millsandboonuk
- 𝕏 @millsandboon

Or get in touch on 0844 844 1351*

For all the latest titles coming soon,
visit millsandboon.co.uk/nextmonth

Want even more
ROMANCE?

Join our bookclub today!

'Mills & Boon books, the perfect way to escape for an hour or so.'

Miss W. Dyer

'Excellent service, promptly delivered and very good subscription choices.'

Miss A. Pearson

'You get fantastic special offers and the chance to get books before they hit the shops'

Mrs V. Hall

Visit millsandbook.co.uk/Bookclub and save on brand new books.

MILLS & BOON